Love in the Age of Bitcoin
Guy Lane

Chapters

Heavy Rain

Heavy rain pummels the rooftops. Strong wind lashes water around in eddies and spirals, dashing against windows and through door seals. Across half the country, the deluge has gone on for days. A large, angry weather system has parked, blocked by upper-level winds that aren't doing what the meteorology textbooks say they should.

In an apartment block in Cherry Tree Lane the gutters are blocked, and rainwater gushes over like a waterfall. This is an old red-brick building, and on the fourth and top floor, a heavy-set man, full of booze is asleep.

Absinthe wakes alone to the sound of his mobile phone receiving a text message. He gasps, laying there, confused staring at the dark ceiling. The sound of the rain is like a constant companion, a low droning thrum. Incessant, ever-present.

As he lays there, wondering why he woke, he becomes conscious of a most noticeable sensation. His heart is pounding so hard that it is almost audible above the sound of the rain. Then he recalls what woke him. An incoming message. Is that the message he has been waiting for? "Is that her?" Has Turtledove sent him a message, at last?

Absinthe fumbles in the dark, searching for the phone but it's not where it ought to be. He has slept fitfully, tossing and turning, anguished by a tormenting dream. The bed sheet is tangled around him. He rises and catches a glimpse of light coming from under the cotton sheet.

The phone sounds again, startling him. Is that the second notification of the first message, or a second message? Maybe Turtledove is in trouble. Absinthe tugs at the sheet, but it is trapped under his body, and he fights against his own weight, exhausting himself.

His heart hammers like the beating rotors of the Bitcrime helicopter. Two days ago he leapt from that chopper into danger but that didn't make him feel as anxious as he does now.

He has the phone in his hand, but it is wrapped in the bed sheet. A cramp forms in his gut as it sounds once again. Is that three messages, now? What dire trouble is Turtledove in?

And then that regular thought, "How long would he survive without her?" It's a valid question, for without her he would be an even bigger mess than he is with her; and it's easy to make deadly mistakes when you work at the pointy end of the Bitcrime Division.

Absinthe sinks his teeth into the sheet and rips it open. He holds the phone away from his face and squints at the screen. He can see words, but he can't read them. His heart speeds and the tension creeps in. His glasses, where the hell are his glasses? He uses the light from the phone to illuminate the small table next to the bed. That's where his glasses should be, but they're not there.

"Damn you!" he hollers, anguished, wracked with anxiety. The phone sounds again, temporarily blocking out the sound of the rain. How many is that? Is that the second notification from the second message? He sweeps his hand under the bed and his fingers graze across an object. He leans over the side of the bed to extend his reach, but the tangled sheet restricts him, and he tumbles onto the floor, crunching his shoulder, and dropping the phone. He grasps the glasses from under the bed only to find that the phone has now dis-illuminated and has disappeared.

Absinthe stumbles out of bed and blindly gropes the walls seeking a light switch. He floods the room with light, revealing a studio apartment heavily lived in. The floor is clear but only because the debris has been shoved to one side. It's a single man's apartment and it has that bachelor pad smell, wet towels and pizza.

He locates the phone, his heart hammering like the barrel of the MP5 machine gun that he fired at the crypto-rats – the energy-wasting cryptocurrency miners – in that noisy warehouse full of hot machines, two days before. The bullets slammed into the crypto-mining rigs in a staccato beat. On the phone, the battery indicator is flashing red, calling for recharge. He opens the messenger app, but in that instant the phone goes flat.

Absinthe grips the phone tightly as he becomes discombobulated with rage. "*Raaaarrrrr!*" He lets out and anguished howl, inhales deeply, and then exhales at length as the moment passes.

Calmer now, he plugs the phone into the charger, conscious of the fact that he has a full five minutes to wait before he can read the message. Fancy failing to plug in the phone. What sort of clown-act is that?

"Get your shit together Absinthe Rhinohorn," he scolds himself.

Absinthe moves into the bathroom sensing the cold air pushing fine drops of rainwater through the gaps in the window frame. He takes stock of his complexion. He's mid-forties and has that look peculiar to men who produce more testosterone than they need. His angular bone structure casts shadows on his face that resemble defilades on a battlefield. Facial hair grows fast and dark, and prickly like barbed wire. Like the safety switch with two settings, his eyes have two settings; doleful or so striking that they can immobilise a man in fear with a single glance.

His dark hair is trimmed number-two-comb on the back and sides but left to grow free on top. Normally, the long hair is swept back and kept in place by the presence of natural oils, but sometimes it gets matted with sweat or blood, and speckled with concrete dust. This is a classic 'Fury Cut', suited to men of war, and practically a fashion statement when compared to number-two all over.

Absinthe stands in front of the mirror, in the cold, swirling air, naked. His strong torso has a thin veneer of chest-hair that goes some ways to hide the scars left behind by shrapnel and the tips of knives. A jagged scar under his armpit was self-inflicted, a drunken unidentified party wound. He's got a few of those.

As for his complexion; in a word, exhausted. Shattered, maybe. Rings under his eyes. Three-day stubble. There is a patch of broken skin on his forehead from when the Monero cryptocurrency mining rig took a bullet and exploded next to his face.

He places his hand on his chest, feeling the heart muscle pounding away. What's that all about? Anxiety about Turtledove's wellbeing? Anxiety about the bollocking he is going to get from his director about the botched mission two days before.

"It's your job to terminate crypto-rats with extreme prejudice," the Bitcrime Director had yelled at him down the phone. "It's your job to destroy the cryptocurrency mining rigs. It is not your job to blow up a fifty-megawatt energy transformer and blackout the city."

Boy, didn't the transformer go up with a bang! The percussion had thrown him off his feet, deafened him temporarily. The rest of his team hospitalised. None killed, thankfully. And all back at work soon after. The transformer had burned, setting fire to the Monero mining rigs, filling the warehouse with acrid smoke.

Maybe that's what's causing the racing heart? There would have been a powerful electromagnetic pulse when the transformer went up. Maybe it had interfered with his pacemaker. That makes sense. The damned pacemaker. But then, where would he be without it? The little electronic device he had worn since he was found to have a defective heart.

One the subject of heart, Turtledove comes back to his thoughts. Where is she? Is she safe? Absinthe becomes gloomy again. Fraught thoughts and mind miles. He looks around the squalid bathroom. How is he faring at being a man who can share his life with a woman? He remembers the lesson, if you're on your own, you need only think about yourself. But if you want someone in your life, you need to apportion a part of your consciousness for them. That's the massage that had been reinforced to him, over and over.

Getting hammered last night and forgetting to plug in the phone is okay alone, but not if you want Turtledove to stay. He observes his facial expression, it's doleful. He glances out of the bathroom and sees the damp, pit of an apartment. Imagine if by some chance Turtledove was rostered to his city and they could get a night together. Is this malodorous man-pad suitable accommodation?

What was that old joke? Absinthe says it aloud, because it amuses him, "I'd never date a woman who'd date a guy like me." He chuckles dryly, but it makes his face hurt and the apartment doesn't get any cleaner. Or drier. Clean the apartment, visit the cardiologist for a pacemaker check. Prepare to get routed in the enquiry into the blown-up transformer. First things first, check the messages.

Calmer now, but with a heart still heavy and running too fast, Absinthe moves back to his bed, raises the phone, and calmly switches it on. Within a minute it is live. He holds his finger over the icon for the messenger app that shows there are two messages. A pang of anxiety flashes. He feels it tingle all the way up his spine and exit the top of his head. He lowers his finger and the app opens.

The messages aren't from Turtledove. Instead, they are from the Director of Bitcrime Division: his boss. The first message says that the inquiry into the blown-up transformer and city-wide blackout has been deferred because they need him back in the field ASAP. That means that there's a new mission on the cards. That's good for him. But is that good for him and Turtledove? And is it okay to be conflicted?

The second message tells him to report to Bitcrime Division HQ at 9am. That's five hours away.

Absinthe lowers the phone, glumly. He ponders for a moment the sentiment that is welling inside him, something that he is compelled to share with Turtledove. He sits there listening to the noise of the raindrops crashing down on the roof. Then he sends Turtledove a message. Just two words, "Be careful."

Planetary Boundaries Diagram

Getting to the office proves to be a much more complicated affair that expected. The rain, falling for a week now, has taken a sudden uptick in intensity. There is now an 'atmospheric river' added into the slow-moving, rain-bearing depression. So says the meteorologist on the radio, who went on to explain that for every degree Celsius that the planet warms, about 7% more water is evaporated into the atmosphere; and all that evaporated water has to go somewhere. Indeed, around the world, it falls in intense bursts, short, sharp, destabilizing hillsides, forcing mudslides and flash floods. Entire villages washed away. Entire cities hosed down; the street gutters flushed of thousands of tonnes of plastic trash washed out to sea. What used to a one in a fifty-year flood, is now an annual event.

You'd really think that people would change their behaviour accordingly but given the most people either don't know or don't care about climate change, the inevitable weather change is just written off, as well.

Absinthe navigates his vehicle through streets greyed-out by the heavy clouds and the incessant rain and watches people literally get washed away in the flood. He pulls up at a set of lights as a stream of water cascades down the street in front of him, a half dozen cars entrained in its watery grip. Fortunately, Absinthe drives a car that is not dissimilar to a small tank, so he is able to navigate the streets without too much bother. When he finally arrives at the office, he is twenty minutes late, but compared to the rest of the people, he is early.

As expected, Absinthe has to endure a bollocking from the Director before he gets to learn about his new mission. The Director is in his sixties, white haired, legally trained and harried by the pressures of his job. The *faux pas* with the transformer only adds to the stress. Fortunately the Director is more bureaucrat that Sergeant Major, so all Absinthe has to do is remain contrite, say "Yes, Sir," and "No, Sir," in the proper order, and he'll get through in no time. At least, that's the plan. In fact, the bollocking plays out rather differently than he had anticipated.

The bollocking begins by the Director drawing his attention to a framed diagram on the wall, a segmented circle with multiple colours. Standing in front of the Director's desk, Absinthe glances at the diagram as instructed.

"I assume that you know what the diagram is," the Director says, beginning his tirade.

"Yes, Sir. I do."

"Would you care to name it so that I can hear you say it in your out-loud voice."

"It's the Planetary Boundaries diagram, Sir."

"Top marks, soldier. But what is it about you that makes me feel the need to do 'Planetary Boundaries for Beginners' every-time you step into my office?"

"I can't answer that, Sir."

"Then answer this. What does that diagram tell us, broadly speaking?"

"It tells us that there are nine global-scale biophysical systems that need to be protected on Earth if the planet is to remain habitable for human beings, Sir."

"Habitable for humans and most of the other species on this planet. Don't forget them."

"Yes, Sir."

"Anything else?"

"Yes, Sir. It tells us that the status of all nine biophysical systems is beyond safe limits."

The Director continues, "And we can intuit that unless there is a significant change in behaviour by the humans, we are on the brink of collapsing the entire living skin of this planet."

"Yes, Sir."

"And our unit, Bitcrime Division, interfaces with which of these nine Planetary Boundaries?"

"Climate Change, Ocean Acidification and Novel Entities, Sir."

"That's correct. So the cryptocurrency miners are hoovering up vast amounts of predominantly coal-fired electricity for absolutely no good purpose, preventing us from meeting our climate change targets, and exacerbating the acidification of the overly hot and dangerously deoxygenated ocean. Plus, they are generating kilo-tonnes of techno-junk in all the defunct mining rigs and associated paraphernalia. And your job is to shoot the crypto-miners and destroy their equipment."

"That's my understanding, Sir."

"All this has to be done on the meagre budgets that the government deigns to give us to save humanity."

"I understand, Sir."

"Oh, do you, Absinthe? Really? And there's all those other Planetary Boundaries have to be protected, too. Our compatriots downstairs in Biosphere Integrity are working very hard to keep the biosphere full of living things other than humans and livestock."

This information is not news to Absinthe. The downstairs department is where Turtledove works. She fights wildlife trafficking in the Pangolin Unit.

"These are all dangerous roles," the Director continues. "They lost three from downstairs just yesterday,"

"Lost? Three?" Absinthe stammers, stunned. Instantly, he is conscious that his heart is hammering away in his chest. His stomach tightens. Was Turtledove killed in action? Is that what the awful dream was, last night? Is that why all he could think to text to her was, "Be careful?"

"It's not the point," the Director snaps. "The point is my frustration."

"Yes, Sir."

"I'd like you to picture my frustration, for a minute, Absinthe. Imagine a man tasked with saving humanity from abrupt climate change and ocean acidification on a shoestring budget, then receiving an invoice from a public utility for $12.6 million to replace the electrical transformer that you absent-mindedly machine-gunned and set on fire, causing a city-wide blackout that lasted an hour and a half. Do you understand how that man might be a bit upset by that, Absinthe Rhinohorn?"

"Yes, Sir." says Absinthe, maybe with just a little less contriteness than was called for as he's still distracted by the news. Turtledove can't have been killed in action because she doesn't go into action. She's a Chief Administrator – a corporate office worker, not a field operative. But maybe the traffickers came for her. Either way, now he's anxious as hell.

"And you'll also understand how frustrated I am that this damned thing should show up in my life." The Director drops a project file on the desk in front of him.

Absinthe recognises the document. It's his new mission.

The Director continues, "It seems that some naughty cryptocurrency miners have found their way into the Centre of Nuclear Technology where there is both a nuclear reactor and a supercomputer that is supposed to be modelling the plume of radioactive water pouring out of the three melted-down cores of the Fukushima Daiichi nuclear power station in Japan. Instead, it is now mining some new cryptocurrency called Hivemind. You need to go there, find the crypto-rats and kill them. But please don't destroy the mining rig, it's very expensive public property."

"Yes, Sir."

"And Absinthe," the Director passes over the project file. "Please don't blow up the nuclear reactor."

"I'll do my very best, Sir." Absinthe turns for the door, but the Director intercepts him.

Up-close, the Director is a bit more Sergeant Major-ish than when seated across the table. Absinthe stiffens as the Director enters his personal space and eyeballs him with a spiteful look. "Let's be clear about something, you and I?" the Director snarls.

"Yes, Sir."

"You're a guy who's named after an alcoholic beverage and an illegal aphrodisiac that doesn't actually work. So it's no wonder you're a drunken, useless fuck."

"Yes, Sir."

"If you cock up another mission, I will personally pour your liquids and powders into a toilet bowl and pull the chain."

"Yes, Sir. Thank you, Sir."

"Well. Good, then," the Director softens. "How's your heart?"

"My heart?" Absinthe feels a surge in his chest.

"There was a powerful EMP burst from that exploding transformer. It could have interfered with your pacemaker."

"I have a good heart, Sir."

"Well, let's hope you have a good career as well."

Get Me That Memo

After the meeting with the Director, Absinthe descends a floor to Department of Biosphere Integrity. Turtledove's unit oversees a heavy-handed response to breaches in the protocols that govern threatened wildlife. From this floor are co-ordinated that activities of researchers and armed wildlife inspectors. Shootouts are common and one of the metrics of success is the body-count of poachers and the members of the organised crime gangs that run them. Sometimes, infrequently, the organised crime gangs proactively take the fight to the Pangolin Unit. This is his fear, that an Asian Triad group has whacked the Pangolin Unit, killing three. It's unlikely, much more likely that a wildlife patrol has lost a firefight.

Turtledove is out of the country, on some stealth mission running covert teams. Last time he saw her, they were stationed in Singapore. At that time, she was organising a hit on a group smuggling tiger penis to Chinese herbalists, and Absinthe was whacking a nest of crypto-miners who had hooked up an extensive Ethereum rig in the basement of a hospital, and were siphoning off three megawatts of mains electricity in the process. The clever little crypto-rats had packed their rigs around the liquefied petroleum gas tanks, threatening to blow up the hospital if the tanks were hit by a stray bullet. Absinthe and his team got around that diversion by cutting power to the facility and invading in the dark with night vision goggles and sharp knives. He'd been with Turtledove for a few hours after the mission, and before he had to fly out to another project. He had asked when he would see her again, and she replied that she didn't know. It didn't seem like the right answer at the time, but now it seems as though it was her way of saying, "I don't know if I will ever see you again."

That is what Absinthe is thinking as he stands at the counter of Biosphere Integrity waiting for a receptionist to attend to him. The young receptionist has seen him and is apprehensive about coming face to face with the sturdy, rugged, gruff kind of man, his heart racing far too fast, a pain gripping his gut, waiting to talk to a stranger about his lover on a secret mission who may be dead. At last the receptionist picks up the courage to address him.

Absinthe composes himself so as not spook the young girl into calling security. "I would like to speak to..." He thinks hard, trying to remember the name of the woman whom he met with Turtledove that night in a bar in Singapore. "Ms Maidmont. Director of..."

"Director Clarence Maidmont?" the girl asks, trembling.

"Yes. That's her."

"And your name is?"

"Absinthe." He wonders if Director Maidmont will remember him by that name, so he completes, "Rhinohorn."

The receptionist puts a call through to the Director's personal assistant. "There is a man here who wants to speak with the Director about rhino horn. Absinthe. His name is Mr Absinthe." She replaces the phone and indicates a seating arrangement, "Please wait."

Absinthe sits, draws a deep sigh and becomes conscious of his heart pummelling away like a drum roll. He is doing the right thing with respect to Turtledove, he thinks. He nods at that. Maybe he's not such a bad catch, after-all.

Finally, the Director's Personal Assistant arrives, and Absinthe follows her through the office. There are hundreds of people on this floor and everywhere you look there are photos of trafficked wildlife: pangolins stuffed into sacks or laid out dead in their hundreds in a burn pit; boxes of baby turtles; a suitcase filled with socks, each containing an endangered parrot, some dead, some alive. The photos are the evidence of the world's unique biodiversity being sold off as fancy pets, ground into libido enhancers, or served up as exotic foods for the wealthy to impress their friends and colleagues. This floor is the world's best chance of slowing down the sixth great extinction of life on Earth – the Sixth Extinction.

Throughout the offices there are photos of dead humans, poachers caught in the act in a forest, on a beach, or trapped inside stifling warehouses packed with sharks fin, elephant tusk, dolphin meat, monkey, and lizard. The photos show dozens of impoverished, desperate people who had no idea of the risks or the ecological implications of what they were doing. These are the pawns of the illegal wildlife trade.

On another wall is a memorial to the fallen members of the Biosphere Integrity team. There are dozens of photos of the deceased, those who gave their lives to protect Earth's wildlife. As he passes this place, Absinthe sees a worker preparing three empty picture frames. His heart races on top of it already racing, expecting to see a photo of Turtledove, ready to be slipped into the empty frame. He halts and asks of the worker, "Who?" but the Director's Personal Assistant becomes surly and ushers him to continue. He follows on, glancing back over his shoulder, desperate for information, but after a few paces, he turns a corner and is directed into a conference room and instructed to sit. And sit he does, stewing in a miasma of anxieties.

Time passes, and he comes to realise that it is being wasted with him mapping out a hundred unlikely scenarios by which Turtledove survived the thing that befell the other three people. He turns his attention to the project file, gripped in his hand. Inside is the intelligence report that tipped off his unit to the Bitcrime.

An indeterminate number of people have been hiving off computational effort from the supercomputer for an uncertain amount of time, mining a new cryptocurrency called Hivemind. There is a document showing reams of code, and a technical analysis scrawled in hand on the side. They'd mined something, then blew their cover when they uploaded to the server. Probably an inside job, Absinthe thinks. They're probably long gone. As a general rule, if you're smart enough to mine crypto on a supercomputer, you're smart enough to figure out how you're going to get caught, and do something to avoid it.

The door opens and Director Maidmont enters. She is suited, brisk, officious, and takes Absinthe by surprise. He recognises her instantly from that night in Singapore, and she recognises him too, although she is visibly surprised.

She sits, clasps her hands and says directly, "I am very busy and I now understand that you are not here to talk about Rhinohorn smuggling."

"I am Rhinohorn."

"Yes. I remember the Singapore Slings. So you are here to talk about...?"

Absinthe knows that she knows what he has come to discuss, but who will be first to break from professional to personal? Clearly not the Director.

Director Maidmont glances down at the open project file and Absinthe is immediately embarrassed. What an incredible breach of professional security. Everything is top secret from everyone else in this place. He folds the cover closed, feeling clownish for having to do so. Time is ticking past in the presence of one who is corporate-busy. He needs to cut to the chase.

Absinthe throws his whole hand on the table, hoping for clemency. "I heard that three people were lost from your unit recently."

Director Maidmont replies with a neutral tone, almost as if she were reading off a pre-prepared script, "That's unsubstantiated scuttlebutt unless you read it in a press release on our official website."

"And when might that be?" Absinthe winces having said this. Too pushy by far. What was he thinking?

"Are you here for a specific reason? Because if you are, I will need a memo from your Director authorising me to disclose confidential information. Are you able to provide that memo, Mr Rhinohorn?"

Absinthe sighs, conscious that he must look like a dishevelled, lovesick dope, trying to prise secrets from a disciplined, professional woman. He has utterly failed to appeal to her on a personal level, and has proved an undisciplined professional himself, having sat there for seconds with a confidential mission profile open in front of a woman who outranks him.

"I'll get that memo," he says, flatly.

"Very well then. Thanks for dropping by." Clarence stands, holds out her hand.

Absinthe shakes, conscious of looking like the way he feels. She opens the door, and escorts him through the offices, talking in general terms about the mission of her department, disclosing nothing that wasn't written on the official website – the website where the death notices are posted. She takes him on a route that bypasses the wall of deceased, and he nearly stumbles as he swivel-necks around, hoping to snare a glance of the pictures in the three new frames.

At the reception counter, Clarence offers her hand again. She says quietly, "I remember the Singapore Slings." Then in her out-loud voice, "Get me that memo."

Those simple words "Get me the memo" resonate through his head as the elevator descends. Get the memo from the guy who thinks of him as a drunken, useless fuck. How's that going to work?

He sighs. The only way that is going to happen is if he can blitz the supercomputer hackers in record time and give the Director a big win, soon. To do that, he needs to read the project file. Ah, yes, the project file. The last time he remembers seeing that thing, it was laying on the desk in front of him. He glances down at his hand and is greatly relieved to see that the document is still there, clenched between his fingers, and that he hasn't somehow dropped it or left it lying in the director's meeting room.

Quantum Entanglement

Back in his hovel-like apartment, Absinthe stands in the doorway drenched from having run from his vehicle parked in the street in front of his apartment.

He looks around the debris of a busy bachelor's life. It's not strewn around the floor like it might have been had he been wholly in the mindset of a single-man. Instead, he has the mindset of a bachelor in transition to a husband. In this instance, the debris is stacked sort-of neatly on the chairs and in the corners. The apartment is definitely cleaner than it was before he cleaned it; albeit only marginally. He considers how such an apartment might be viewed from the perspective of Turtledove, assuming that the poor girl still existed, that is. He is unable to answer that question definitively, but he thinks that she would - at the very least - acknowledge that he was 'trying'. That's got to be worth something in relationship terms, surely.

Absinthe sits on the side of his bed and opens the messenger app on his phone. He stares forlornly at the message he sent earlier that morning "Be careful." How did that turn out, he wonders?

Then he becomes conscious of his overly beating heart again. What is it with that damned muscle? Is that stress? Loneliness? Or a malfunction in the electronic device that controls its rhythm? Or maybe it's just love in the age of Bitcoin.

Absinthe thinks back to his plan to visit the cardiologist to have the software in his pacemaker checked. How was that crucial, life-saving plan going? Lost in the duties of the day. Maybe tomorrow. Probably not, as he has a bunch of cryptos-rats to flush out of a nuclear-powered supercomputer so that he can get a memo from the director who thinks of him as a drunken, useless fuck. Absinthe sighs.

Conscious of not wanting to bug Turtledove who is pretty-much always corporate-busy, assuming that she was still extant and able to be bugged, he sends another text message that simply reads, "I you."

On first glance to a normal person, this might seem a rather trivial combination of a few short words. But in reality, it was the most profound outpouring of empathy that is possible between two human beings. What was intended by the message was that Absinthe was 'feeling' Turtledove. Feeling, not in the physical sense, but in the sensing sense. He was enmeshed with her, in the way that photons become entangled in a quantum physics kind of way. In that what happens to an entangle photon over here happens to its entangled mate over there.

Or something like that. How was he to know? After all, what would Absinthe Rhinohorn know about the intersection of quantum physics and love? He was a simple grunt whose job was to flush out and eradicate cryptocurrency miners. He was more hammer than neuron. More brute force than intelligence. What could he know about love except that it felt good, and it hurt, and both of these things felt natural in an odd, confusing sort of way?

Absinthe stares at the phone, noticing that the two most recent pieces of communication between him and his lover were both from him, and consisted of no more than four words: "Be careful, I you."

Is that the correspondence of a good catch, he wonders? Does that add currency to their emotional bank account? He lowers the phone, feeling like it isn't yielding the response that he was yearning for, i.e. a reply.

On the table, he sees the project file. He reluctantly shuffles over to it and opens its cover. He sits there for some moments listening to the sound of the rain, unable to concentrate. Finally, he gets back in his professional flow, doing his research to help him root out and eradicate cryptocurrency miners.

Catch the Rats Alive

For Absinthe and his team of thuggish looking companions, the trip to the Centre for Nuclear Technology is a three-hour ride in a chopper powered by carbon-neutral algae biofuel. The chopper produces an exhaust trail that smells of fresh popcorn, an exhaust that leaves no net carbon in the atmosphere.

The team are dressed in military body armour, brandishing a suite of lethal and non-lethal weapons. This is the pointy end of Bitcrime Division and the group motto is: Stay Sharp. Accompanying them are three nerdy-looking types who are specialists in cryptocurrency software. They are exhausted, having spent days pouring over the code that had been extracted from the hacked supercomputer. Very odd it was, almost unintelligible, except that one of the code writers had foolishly showed his hand by adding technical notes in amongst the long strings letters and numbers. One such note advised the name of the code: Hivemind. This lead the Bitcrime nerds to a white-paper published years ago that described a mechanism to mine cryptocurrency on the Internet of Things, thus enabling the hackers to crypto-mine pretty-much every device on the planet that was connected to the internet. That included every photocopier, printer, refrigerator, anything. This threat had been discussed for years, and now it had become real. While it may sound innocuous, the implication is that energy demand would shoot up everywhere the Hivemind was activated, frustrating attempts to cut carbon at the risk of overheating the world through abrupt climate change. The big question remains. If Hivemind was designed to mine on small things, why had it been allowed to infect something as huge as a super-computer? None of the technical people had an answer for that.

Amongst the Bitcrime division crew there are different views on abrupt climate change. Helmet is a beefy brute with a peroxide blonde flat top. He has a face that resembles a bare-knuckle pugilist who stayed in the game for too long. He's a doomer who thinks that the planet has already crashed through the climate tipping points, and that the demise of 8 billion humans and most other living species is imminent. "The Pickle Point was years ago," he'd often say. "I'm surprised we're still here."

The Pickle Point is the moment when you realise that you've gone past the tipping-point, and you are now in free-fall. It's like that moment when Wile E. Coyote, having rushed off the cliff in the pursuit of the Road Runner, spins his legs in mid-air, hovers magically in cartoon anti-gravity for a few seconds, before glancing at the camera, and then plummeting to the ravine floor, below. The glance at the camera, that occurs at the Pickle Point. It comes with an automatic need to share.

When once asked if, given that he felt that way, why didn't he go live on a beach and blow cones all day, Helmet replied, "I'm just looking for a little payback." Another time, drunk on rum, he admitted that he just liked killing crypto-miners.

Another member of the team is Carly. She's kind of hot looking. A former dancer with Cirque du Soleil, males are well advised not to get a boner around her when she's carrying an MP5 submachine gun because she is one deadly bitch. She doesn't really understand all the scientific stuff about climate change. She works at the pointy end of Bitcrime Division because she gets to dress and act like John Rambo. She's got a thing for lipstick lesbians and chicks dig all that Rambo shit.

On the subject of abrupt climate change, Horace, the third member of the group, is an Interventionist. He's the intellectual who always has his head in a book or some technical paper on Earth Science. An Interventionist is a person who believes that doom is not inevitable, but it will be unless there is an intervention in the way that humans conduct themselves on Earth. Given that there is no magic bullet technology, happy human-loving intervening God, or a trillionaire spacemen coming to the planet's rescue, Interventionists try to do the intervening, themselves. Typically, they are obsessive workaholics with an unnerving can-do attitude. These are people that focus on a singular pursuit, generally to the detriment of all other aspects of their lives. Horace does nothing besides research and work Bitcrime Division. Occasionally, he drinks rum with Helmet.

On the subject of abrupt climate change, Absinthe doesn't really have an opinion. He doesn't even know why he does his job; he just does it and does it well - except for blowing up the expensive transformer, that is. He can't recall when he started the job. All he remembers is a long blur of fire-fights, cryptocurrency rigs blowing up, bodies flying through the air, punctuated by intense drinking sessions and hangovers, and the occasional broken heart. Absinthe doesn't really think about much, at all. He's more a doer than a thinker.

All that said, at this point in time, as the chopper purrs through the sky, Absinthe is intently contemplating two interconnected ideas. First, he is conjuring up a suite of plausible scenarios by which Turtledove could be alive and well, and simply unable to reply to his text messages. If she fails to reply soon, and there is no press release on the Biosphere Integrity website naming three other dead operatives, he'll have no choice but to go to Plan B to confirm her proof of life. He'll have to approach the Director of Bitcrime Division who thinks he's a drunken, useless fuck, and ask him to write a memo requesting classified information from the other Director whom he is sure thinks of him as little more than an unprofessional, dishevelled, lovesick dope. Absinthe crunches the numbers on that for a little while and concludes that Plan B is looking a bit shaky, right now. That said, if he returns quickly from the nuclear place having liquidated the crypto-rats, and he can make it look as though the Director has single-handedly saved the entire fucking Universe, maybe the memo won't be such a big deal after-all.

Absinthe is alerted to a sound from the cockpit. He turns to see the Co-pilot holding fingers in the air. Touch-down in four minutes. He nods, and the Co-pilot turns back to his controls.

The enigma of the Supercomputer running Hivemind is not lost on Absinthe, and he mulls over how it necessarily affects the *modus-operandi* for the current mission. Normally, there is no mystery to be solved with the crypto-miners; they are just making personal gain at everyone else's expense, and they get liquidated accordingly. This supercomputer thing is different. There is no way the Director will come out a hero if that mystery is left unresolved.

Absinthe checks his watch and raises three fingers to his crew: three minutes to touch-down. Then he says aloud, "We have to catch these rats alive."

Don't Blow Up the Reactor

With the pace of his heartbeat rising and falling in an inexplicable pattern, Absinthe leads his team of hard-asses and nerds to the office of the Director of the Centre of Nuclear Technology. The secretary is visibly shocked to see the armed Bitcoin Division operatives, and she anxiously shows them through to the Director's office. Inside, Absinthe realises that he has seen quite enough of Directors recently, so he leaves Horace in charge of the investigation. He addresses the waiting Head of Security and demands a full tour of the facility.

Absinthe and Helmet reconnoitre the nuclear facility with the Head of Security telling them a bunch of things that they already know because the pointy end of Bitcrime Division does a whole shit-pile of research before they go looking for crypto-rats. They visit the place where the crypto-rats hooked the supercomputer to a modem and uploaded their illegally mined data. The supercomputer occupies a huge hall that is brightly illuminated and immaculately clean. Hundreds of dark grey cabinets with panels of twinkling lights are laid out with geometrical precision forming an oval-shaped spiral. The room hums with the sound of thousands of cooling fans, and the air is tinged with the smell of pine floor cleaner and the ozone that is emitted from the hot electrical boards.

Then Absinthe has the security guy show him around the nuclear reactor. It is a monstrous machine inside a huge, multi-storey building. The cavernous containment dome reminds Absinth of a gothic cathedral, the sense of a vast, enclosed space and looming doomsday. The nuclear reactor itself is a gigantic steel contraption with cables and pipes arrayed with such precise complexity, it almost looks like it had grown out of metal. They enter the containment dome at a mid-level, and the reactor, surrounded by metal decking, stretches a dozen floors above and below.

"Show me subsection 14A," Absinthe gruffly instructs the security guy, referring to the place that he and Horace had resolved was the weak spot, the place where a small explosive charge would trigger the nuclear reactor to vigorously explode. As they walk along a long corridor, the oppressive sound of the nuclear power station rumbles through the surrounding concrete. Huge pumps whirr, pushing great volumes of cooling water. A steam turbine howls, spinning and pumping out 500 megawatts of base-load mains electricity.

Now, technically, electricity from a nuclear plant has no carbon footprint because no fossil fuels are burned. This means that crypto-mining using nuclear powered electricity is carbon neutral. However, given that electricity networks are interconnected, any additional electricity demand raises the carbon footprint across the whole electricity system because there are coal plants dotted throughout the network. And given that crypto-mining provides zero benefit except to those crypto-rats that mine it, and that there are other ways to generate cryptocurrency without mining – Proof of Stake, for example - there really is no saving the crypto-rats once the pointy end of Bitcrime Division catches up with them.

Absinthe sends Helmet and the Head of Security ahead to the next venue, and stands at subsection 14A, looking at the wall of the reactor vessel. He glances around to see that no-one is watching, and then slides back the cocking arm on his MP5 submachine gun, flicks the safety off, and raises the barrel to the metal. His finger rests lightly on the trigger and he inhales deeply, closing his eyes. He concentrates, feeling the rhythm of his heart. It is hammering away as it has been for days, over-exerting itself. But there is no change in its beat as he raises his rifle. Clearly, the pace of his heart is not created by danger stress. It's either a corrupted pacemaker. Or maybe it is love in the age of Bitcoin.

His eyes closed, gun muzzle resting against the reactor, he thinks about Turtledove. He remembers when he first laid eyes on her. It was at a conference that explored the intersection of cryptocurrencies and wildlife poaching. You see, some cryptocurrencies are completely untraceable. They enable completely anonymous transactions, which is what the poachers want, so they can annihilate Earth's biodiversity with impunity.

Absinthe remembers the first instant that he saw Turtledove. He glanced her as she walked past in the busy auditorium. The effect was instant. He turned, his jaw dropped, and he watched as she was enveloped by the crowd. Absinthe stood that way, statue-like, for minutes, stunned by the petite, black-haired woman. He caught two other fleeting glimpses of her that day and finally found her standing alone at the after-conference buffet.

Holding a flute of French champagne and wearing a blue cocktail dress, she dipped a tiger prawn in thousand islands dressing. Absinthe approached as she ate the prawn. He had a well-rehearsed opening line but found himself mute when he came within a few feet of her. So Turtledove spoke instead and told him about the eleven elephants that were now back in the stream, having been rescued from poachers by the Pangolin Unit. She told him other happy stories, cleverly prising the good news out of the mountain of woe that was the wildlife poaching business, like a diamond miner finds gems amongst the alluvial pebbles in a stream. It all grew from there, really. They were clearly so different, but for a time, the circles of their Venn diagram overlapped sufficiently to overcome the forces that pulled them apart.

It seemed so wrong to Absinthe that someone as lovely as Turtledove should have to share the world with something as odious as elephant poachers and pangolin smugglers. He had always felt that his involvement in her life had somehow counteracted that sad truth; that he could protect her from all the bad things. Or at least distract her from it, periodically.

Absinthe sighs, how he misses her, and how complicated it is to spend time with her. His sigh breaks him from his contemplative trance, and he finds himself standing in front of a nuclear reactor with a loaded submachine gun pointed at the weak spot. A thought comes to his mind. If he learns that he will never see her again, he will return to this place, and bring with him a bigger gun. And armour piercing bullets.

Absinthe de-arms his weapon and steps away from the reactor vessel. For a moment he is pensive, thinking it through. Then he realises that somehow, miraculously, he has survived. His inclination towards self-inflicted extinction has avoid one more time.

He goes to find Helmet and the security guy, then walks at a pace with them to Horace and Carly. In the mess hall, he sits with his team and listens to the debriefing.

Ventilate Their Brainstems

Absinthe listens intently as Horace briefs him on his interpretation of events regarding the hacked supercomputer. The script that overwrote the supercomputer code, forcing it to mine Hivemind, was probably written by a team, based elsewhere. A single operative was likely all was needed to install the software and then three days later facilitate the supercomputer to upload the mined data to an encrypted proxy server. The identities of the recipients of the data transfer would likely never be known due to the nature of the encryption. "It's been totally Moneroed," Horace says. As for what the crypto-rats had actually mined, that too is a mystery.

The one lead they had was the identity of the likely technician who managed the hack inside the facility. One member of the supercomputer team had suspiciously called in sick the day after the upload and the hack was discovered. He had a local address, which was false, but Horace had pinged him via biometrics, put the word out on the wire and got a response from Interpol who said that the guy had a prior. Interpol provided Horace with an address which could be a possible bolt hole.

"My recommendation," Horace completes his debrief. "I say we that we chopper there now and ventilate his brainstem."

"Sounds good to me," says Helmet, slapping his meaty palms together.

"We catch these guys alive," Absinthe says, thinking of the memo.

"Alive?" asks Carly, taken aback. "What for?"

"So we can ventilate him later," says Helmet.

They all laugh, except for Absinthe Rhinohorn who is now feeling compromised, as he realises that he is blending his personal life into his work, something that is generally recognised as leading to a bad outcome, because it's easy to make life-threatening mistakes when distracted at the pointy end of Bitcrime Division.

"Alive!" he says authoritatively, then realises just how out of character that is. So he backs it up with a rational justification. "We have to get to the bottom of the mystery. Why are they mining Hivemind on a supercomputer? We need to interrogate a suspect."

"And ventilate him later," says Carly.

And thus, the plan was formed. The bolt-hole is a thirty-minute chopper ride away, in the mountains, in an abandoned hydro-power station. The pointy end of Bitcrime Division departs the mess hall in the Centre of Nuclear Technology and step into their waiting chopper.

Not Taken Lightly

As the chopper approaches the mountain, the thermal camera picks up the cool plume of the river and a hotspot, the tell-tale sign of a crypto mine's ventilation tube. The chopper hovers over the vent, the back ramp descends, and a thick, black rope is tossed out the back.

"Rules of engagement?" Helmet asks as he grips the rope in both hands, ready to slide into the danger zone.

"Engage only if they engage. I want the brains alive," Absinthe growls.

The four members of the Bitcrime Division abseil from the chopper into the crypto exhaust pipe. They slide rapidly along the pipe, not knowing what they will find at its end. The sensation of being inside the ventilation tube is exhilarating; a high-pitched whine of a thousand fans, and the stench of ozone in the hot air bursting around them.

They fall through the ceiling of a crypto mining farm housed inside a concrete chamber dug into the hillside, landing right in the middle of a mixed, high-density complex of crypto-rigs. There's a bank of Ant-miners on metal racks chomping through hundreds of kilowatts of electricity generated by the refurbished hydropower station. Hanging from cables in the ceiling are a thousand or so Nvidia graphics CPUs, probably mining some new crypto that hasn't yet raised in value enough for the difficulty to set in and raise the computational effort of mining its hash.

The four members of the pointy end of Bitcrime Division scan the scene for signs of crypto-rats. The first evidence is a staccato beat of automatic weapons fire, the bullets flying over their head, slamming into the ceiling and filling the air with concrete dust. Instantly, Bitcrime Division swoops into action, guns blazing. Carly strafes the mining rigs, causing them to explode in a burst of cables, wires, hot CPUs and bright green sparks. Helmet stomps forward toward the assailant and floors him with a burst of metal from his MP5. Two other crypto-rats leap up from a workstation. One grabs a laptop computer, the other a mini-Uzi machine pistol, they both run down the hallway towards the turbines of the hydro-power station. Helmet and Absinthe give chase.

The guy with the Uzi turns and fires. Helmet strafes in his direction and three rounds entering and exit his torso. He falls, and Absinthe kicks the gun from his dying hand as he swoops past. The third, unarmed, crypto-rat leaps over a piece of machinery, turns abruptly right, and disappears from view.

Helmet belts around the corner after him, finding himself in a smaller tunnel with a dead end. The only thing in the tunnel is a porta-loo. Helmet opens up with his MP5 on full-auto putting eight rounds into the centre of the door. No sooner had the spent casings hit the floor than Absinthe catches up and sees the shot-up porta-loo.

Absinthe pushes open the bullet ridden dunny door with the barrel of his MP5 submachine gun. He glances inside at the mess. There is more blood on the walls than in the crypto-miner, which is generally a sign of a job well done, and that it's time to knock-off and have a coldie beer. The scene reminds Absinthe of the pictures of the shot-up poachers in the Biosphere Integrity department. And he remembers being admonished by the Director to get him the memo. Well you can forget any complicity from Bitcrime Director now. Turtledove seems to have become even more distant and unreachable. And it's all Helmet's fault. Absinthe turns, sees him smirking.

"Oops," Helmet says, theatrically.

Enraged, Absinthe rushes him, crushing a forearm against Helmet's throat. "I said keep them alive!" Absinthe lashes Helmet's face with hot spittle.

"Settle petal," Helmet grimaces.

But Absinthe doesn't settle because he can't; he's absolutely livid. This isn't about breaking orders and ventilating the crypto-rat. This is about the *pragmacticalities* the pragmatic practicalities - of defending Turtledove; doing what needs to be done!

"He's killing him!" shouts Carly rushing into the scene and stunned to see Helmet's face going quite blue. Horace leaps onto Absinthe's back and tears him away from the half-strangled Helmet. Absinthe leans forward, tossing Horace on top of Helmet against the wall. Carly races in to immobilize Absinthe, but he over-powers her, too, and she is sent sprawling onto the deck.

Absinthe clasps the grip of his MP5 submachine gun and strafes the wall above the heads of his three companions. The sound of the gunfire is intense in the narrow tunnel, the bullets zinging past their ears and slamming into the concrete wall. Chips of concrete fly out in all directions as Absinthe empties the 30-round magazine, zig-zagging a trail of bullets close to their heads.

When the MP5 runs out, he ditches the long gun, pulls out his Glock pistol and continues to shoot the wall bringing the bullets closer and closer to his team-members heads. He pumps out twelve rounds then stops firing, keeping the final three bullets to execute every mother-fucking last one of them, if needs be.

Horace, Helmet and Carly look up from their position, cowering on the floor to see Absinthe has the pistol trained on them. Their mouths are filled with concrete dust, their ears ringing.

Absinthe yells in a booming, gravelly voice, "I am not a...!"

He doesn't complete his sentence, but they all know what he means. The violent spectacle of machine gunning a hole in the wall close to his team-mates' heads was an Absinthe Rhinohorn way of saying: "I'm not a man who takes insubordination lightly, so please follow orders."

A Memo Encoded

The following morning at 9am, Absinthe is back in front of the Bitcrime Director's desk, standing to attention while the Director reviews the project file that Horace had been up all-night writing. During that same night, Rhinohorn had been drinking heavily, trying desperately not to send distracting or inappropriate texts to Turtledove, who has still not replied to his previous two heart-felt missives. He'd also exerted considerable mental energy trying to ascertain the best way to get the Bitcrime Director to agree to send the memo that he had written out and printed while he was still sober.

Absinthe stands there, looking at the wall while the Director browses the report making satisfied, "*Ahhh*" and "*Uh-Hum*" noises. He chortles at length when he comes to the photos of the ventilated crypto-rat in the porta-loo.

Absinthe's heart is churning like a washing machine full of combat fatigues as he thinks about the one text message that he had been 'unable-to-not-send' to Turtledove the night before. He doesn't remember sending it, he found it when he woke in the morning. Blackout, they call that; it's an alcoholic thing. He's been stressing about the text message for hours now, going back and forth whether it was stupid or smart or something in-between.

One minute he thinks that the text message may have triggered an extinction-level event in his relationship with Turtledove, and his stomach cramps at the thought. The next minute he's thinking it was a bit of harmless fun, that she'll see the message, have a quick 'lol' then get back to being corporate-busy, and that overall it will add capital to the emotional bank account that they both share. And another minute again he actually thinks it's quite clever as it so neatly sums up what he was thinking at that particular moment in time, a combination of lust and love and the need for extreme brevity in communication. And the next minute he thinks it is a ridiculous over-share which takes him back to regretting sending the text.

'Post-wine', that's the official name for correspondence sent after inebriation has set in. It was sent at 2am, Absinthe's witching hour. This is the time when really weird shit normally happens in his life.

What did the text message say? It said this: "I want you to suck my love you."

How embarrassing would it be to have to have to explain the motivation behind that message, Absinthe thinks?

The Director completes his review of the case file and interrupts Absinthe from his miasmatical anxieties by saying, "So, Rhinohorn finally shows up in the relationship."

"The relationship, Sir?"

"Our relationship. Which is doing very nicely, right now. In less than forty-eight hours from receiving the hacked Supercomputer mission, Rhinohorn identifies the perpetrators, tracks them to a mountain redoubt, ventilates them with MP5s, and destroys their crypto-rig. In so doing, he provides a hero-shot of a crypto-rat overtly ventilated in a porta-loo holding a laptop computer with a bullet hole right through the middle of the hard-drive. 'Good work Rhinohorn' just doesn't seem to do it justice."

"I am happy to make you look good, Sir."

"And I am happy that you are happy that you make me look good. That said, there is one very significant missing piece of this crypto-jigsaw."

"What is that Sir?"

"Well, from what I read in this excellently written report, these crypto-rats were mining Hivemind on a supercomputer, when Hivemind is a cryptocurrency designed for the small stuff on the Internet of Things. How do you explain that anomaly, Mr Rhinohorn?"

"It's an interesting quirk with little relevance to a successful mission, Sir."

The Director seems content with that answer, "And the bullet-ridden dunny door is a lovely touch. I might requisition that for the Bitcrime Museum."

"Very good, Sir. Will that be all, Sir?"

"That's all, Soldier, until there's more." The Director waves him away and returns his attention to the photos in the report.

Absinthe hesitates to move, trapped in indecision about whether he ought to follow through on his plan with the memo.

The Director looks up, then steps up from the desk and moves into Absinthe's personal space. "Rhinohorn is still here. Why?"

"I have a request."

"You have a request of me?" the Director is clearly surprised.

"Yes, Sir. I'd like you to fax a memo from your office."

"Really, now? And who would you like to fax the memo to?"

"I can't tell you." Absinthe hands over the folded piece of paper and watches as the Director browses the words.

The memo is addressed to the fax number of the Director of Biosphere Integrity. It is labelled as being from Bitcrime Directorate, and it contains the following words, "re turtledove send proof alive ASAP to Rhinohorn," and it completes with his own mobile phone number.

The Director studies the memo intently, trying to make sense of it. "It's meaningless," he concludes shaking his head.

"It's encrypted, Sir."

"Well, what would it say decrypted?"

"I can't tell you, Sir."

"So you want me to send a fax with an unknown message to an unidentified person? Really, Absinthe?"

"I know what it means."

"Then tell me."

"I can't."

"You can't or you won't."

"I won't."

"Don't forget who you fucking work for! I order you!"

"It's not work related."

"So, it's personal."

"Yes, Sir."

Absinthe remains at attention while the Director wears a perturbed look and mutters aloud, trying to figure it out.

The Director shuffles closer. "Rhinohorn, let me very clear with you about one thing."

"Yes, Sir."

"I am not your friend. I am your director. You work for me and you do as I say or I replace you. That is the totality and extent of our relationship. There is nothing else. Do you understand?"

"Yes, Sir."

The Director folds the note and slides it into Absinthe's breast pocket. "So why don't you take your cryptic Turtledove memo and get the fuck out of my office?"

Pinged by the Guards

Absinthe descends a floor in the elevator, feeling as though his life has come adrift. All his plans to obtain Turtledove proof-alive have come to naught. He simply does not know what to do next. This is a dangerous situation because when Absinthe Rhinohorn doesn't know what to do, pretty-much anything could happen. He steps into the reception area of Biosphere Integrity - the division where Turtledove either works or worked - and bangs his hand against the bell on the receptionist desk. The noise rings out, signalling to everyone on the floor that Absinthe wants answers. A door opens a fraction, and Absinthe sees the young receptionist girl coming to tend him. As soon as she sees him, she retreats and closes the door behind her.

"Strange," thinks Absinthe. He hits the bell again, reminding everyone that he has yet to receive satisfaction. He stands there without a plan, all alone in the world with no one to hear his anxious request.

Shortly, the door opens behind him, and he turns to see two security guards in uniform looking at him wearily, their hands resting on their service pistols.

"Just take it easy, Sir," one of the guards says, holding his free hand out. "No need to get hurt."

"You must know someone I don't know," Absinthe growls. He doesn't know why he has been pinged but pinged he has most certainly been. "What to do?" he wonders. Fight, flight or go quietly with the armed men. He knows that if he escalates the situation in the reception area then all of his Biosphere Integrity privileges, such that he actually has any, will be lost. So he chooses to go quietly. At least for now.

He raises his hands above his head and walks backwards towards the two poorly trained armed men.

"Let's talk about this in the basement," he instructs his two arresting officers with such conviction that they immediately comply. They shuffle backwards towards the elevator the doors slide open and all three step inside. Yes, three men step into an elevator from which only one will emerge standing.

On the basement floor, the elevator doors slide open, and Absinthe steps over the collapsed bodies of the unconscious security guards, into the car park. A second passes and the thought comes to his mind again about Turtledove. Is she still alive? What does he have to do to find out? And then, at the very moment that the elevator doors close and take the unconscious security guards to a higher floor, leaving Absinthe alone in the bleak concrete carpark, something truly amazing happens.

She's right there, right in front of him. Turtledove. She's right there.

A car pulls up, a black VW SUV. The tinted window of the passenger seat rolls down revealing Turtledove seated inside. She's wearing a beige overcoat, her long black hair resting on the shoulders. Absinthe is stunned to see her angelic face, her wry smile, and he becomes conscious of his heart pummelling like the sound of a herd of stampeding wild horses.

Absinthe glances into the cabin of the car to see that the driver is Clarence Maidmont, the Director of Biosphere Integrity, the woman who requested but didn't receive his memo that has been printed but not sent. Director Maidmont says, "Here is Turtledove proof alive."

"You've hurt yourself," Turtledove reaches out her hand to touch the skin on Absinthe's forehead next to where the fragments of the exploding Monero mining rig struck him. "I'm sorry I couldn't return your messages," she says. "Particularly that last one."

"Can I see you?" Absinthe is aware of the tone of his voice. It is that of a desperate man asking for charity? Or is it the sound of a proud man setting up a rendezvous with his lover? Probably a bit of both, really.

"I can come to you at nine. But only for a short while."

Absinthe nods. He takes Turtledove's small hand and places it against his cheek. It feels like a scented flower against his skin.

"How's your heart?" Turtledove asks. But Absinthe doesn't know how to answer, and all he can do is take a step back as the tinted electric window rolls up and Turtledove disappears from view. He stands there watching the vehicle move on, turn a corner and move out of sight. For a moment he is stunned, disbelieving that his fortune had changed so dramatically. Did that just happen?

A powerful wave of release sweeps over him as he realises that not only is Turtledove alive but that their relationship is such that she will night-visit him. All the stress and anxiety of Turtledove proof alive is washed away in a wave euphoria. It is numbing and all-encompassing but it doesn't last long before he is gripped by angst. There is so much to do in the next 11 hours, visit the cardiologist, clean the apartment. Yes, clean the apartment.

Absinthe is distracted by a noise behind him. He turns to see the elevator doors open. Inside, a kind stranger helps one of the battered security guards to his feet. Absinthe takes this as a sign that he should get on his way, and he moves quickly through the basement to his car.

Dr Stent, Cardiologist

Most patients need to book ahead to get to see Dr Stent, the Cardiologist, but Absinthe has special privileges in the heart clinic, and so he just shows up. At the reception, the girls aren't afraid of him like they are at Biosphere Integrity. The girl who checks him in even has a special smile for him. She's got a mop of fawn coloured hair and a plain, but pretty face.

"There you go, Mr Randy Horn," she says with a cheeky grin as she directs him to sit.

Absinthe doesn't pick up on her lascivious word play as he is still processing having seen Turtledove alive. He sits and waits for the cardiologist, conscious of his heart thrumming like the engine of a ship pushing through heavy seas.

Finally, Dr Stent arrives and begins his medical examination in the very waiting room. Absinthe looks up as the doctor places his hand on the soldier's heart and says, "There is something wild in there."

Absinthe has his second flush of catharsis for the day, feeling the anxiety about his over-beating heart being immediately relieved by the expert hands of the cardiologist.

"Let's get you into the machine and see what's going on in there."

Shortly, Absinthe is laying in the heart machine, topless. Cables are connected to his flesh and the machine whirrs over-head. He glances up to see the cheeky receptionist in the doorway looking at him. She raises her hand to make a little wave. This causes Absinthe to smile. It's all a bit odd. He sees that she wears a name tag, but he hadn't thought to see what her name was when he was standing close to her.

The heart machine whirs away and Dr Stent "*Umms*" and "*Ahhs*" as he ponders over the results. Eventually, he has Absinthe sit, and he shares his new knowledge.

"So, Absinthe, there seems to be nothing wrong with your heart, physically. But it is certainly beating way too fast. Have you a lot of stress on right now?"

"Just the normal stress from ventilating crypto-rats, I guess. And I thought that my girlfriend was dead for about three days."

"Oh, you have a girl-friend?" Dr Stent is surprised.

"Well, I guess."

"So, do you have a girlfriend, or do you 'not' have a girlfriend? It's yes or no, Absinthe. It's binary."

"It's more quantum than that," Absinthe thinks. He replaces his shirt, trying to answer the question in the yes or no sort of way. He thinks through the facts. There is a girl who for a while took his calls late at night. There is a girl who slept with him numerous times. There is a girl for whom he has strong emotional feelings. And there is a girl making a night-visit, tonight. So yes, Absinthe has a girlfriend, and her name is Turtledove. The question that comes to mind is, does Turtledove have a boyfriend called Absinthe Rhinohorn? That, he can't tell. "Yes, I have a girlfriend," he tells the cardiologist.

"*Uh-huh*," says Dr Stent. "Now this is very interesting." He tilts the computer monitor so that Absinthe can see a tangle of code scrolling down. "This is the source code from your pacemaker. The pacemaker seems to functioning properly, but there is a block of code in there that shouldn't be. Maybe that's what making the pacemaker trigger your contractions more frequently than it ought.

"How did that code get there?"

"I don't know. Maybe it is a bit of source code replicated and corrupted by that electromagnetic pulse you described from the exploding transformer. Or maybe it's…" Dr Stent's voice trails away as he studies the script.

"Or maybe it's what?"

"Or maybe it's something else. I'll run an analysis and get some results back to you tomorrow. Meantime, I am going to delete this unnecessary code, and let you get back to your life."

"So my heart is okay?" asks Absinthe, meekly.

"Your heart's fine. You pacemaker is fine. And now the source code is fine. Now you can get on and enjoy the heartbeat of a man who works a high-stress job with guns, who drinks like a dipsomaniac, and who has a nasty case of lovesickness."

"Lovesick?"

"Yes, lovesick. It's very common. It's normally transmitted sexually. Fortunately, it's not permanent, and it generally goes away on its own, in good time."

"How do you know this?" Absinthe asks, disarmed.

"I am not just a scholar of the physiology of the heart," Dr Stent tells him rather too plainly. "I also study the emotional aspects that people associate with the heart."

Absinthe nods blankly, taking it all in.

"If you can't answer yes or no to the simple question, 'Do you have a girlfriend?' then there is obviously a lot of stressy emotional stuff sloshing around in there with all the bourbon or rum or whatever it is that you anaesthetize yourself with, nightly. Try to get some resolution to that question, Absinthe. It will take the pressure off your heart."

Undies on the Chair

Turtledove arrives at 9pm sharp. Absinthe pulls open the door to see her standing there. She's wearing the same beige overcoat, pale pink lipstick, and a concerned frown. She holds a bottle of red wine and her handbag. She steps into the room and Absinthe closes the door behind her. Inside the apartment, alone at last, Absinthe wraps her in a smothering embrace that dwarfs her (comparatively) tiny body. She is unable to respond because her arms are trapped, but she does manage to flap the wine bottle against Absinthe's side, a cross between an affectionate pat and tapping out of a cage fight.

When Absinthe releases his hug, he sees that Turtledove is wry-smiling again. He can't know that that smile is because she finds him pug-funny; his emotional intensity a little pathetic sometimes. "Oh, you've had a wee clean in your apartment," she says airily, placing her bag on a pile of newspapers on the kitchen table.

Absinthe looks around proudly. The apartment did scrub up alright, really. All the stuff that was spread randomly over there is now stacked efficiently over here. He'd done a bit of a mop in the kitchen. He is reminded of this because the mop and bucket are sitting in the middle of the lounge room.

"And you've even have a wee flower."

Ahhh, yes, the flower. He is glad that she noticed. Rhinohorn the romantic, does it again! He'd found a plastic flower under the sink when he was looking for floor cleaning products. It was a bit grubby, but he rinsed it and set it in a mug full of water on the kitchen table, next to the pile of newspapers.

She holds out the bottle of red wine, "I'd like a wee glass now, if that's alright."

Absinthe takes the bottle to the kitchen and fossicks around for a corkscrew and clean glasses. *Ahhh*, yes. Clean glasses. He'd forgotten about them.

"So how have you been, Absinthe?" Turtledove calls out, listening to him furtively washing wine glasses in the sink.

How has he been? Good question, really. He's been out of his mind with worry, convinced that his sweetheart had been massacred by a Chinese organised-crime gang. He'd jeopardised his job twice by making inappropriate requests of Directors. He'd come close to shooting his own team members to death because he was falling apart. He'd drunk himself into oblivion every night to numb the pain. He'd come across a fascinating insight: that he had a girlfriend, although he didn't know whether his girlfriend had him as a boyfriend, in return; and he's been stressing about that all afternoon. That's how he's been.

He returns to the main-room with the two clean glasses. Turtledove has moved a pair on undies off the chair and has seated herself at the table.

He hands her a glass and, as he pours the wine, he responds to her question, "Busy, I guess. I had to ventilate some crypto-rats in the mountains, the other day. It's nice up there."

"Whoa. That's enough." Turtledove halts his wine pouring when her glass is a quarter full.

"Are you sure?"

"Yes. I can only stay for a little while."

"Really?" Absinthe's disappointment is palpable.

"They bought me in for a debriefing, and they're putting me straight back in, undercover," Turtledove tells him.

"What have you been working on?" Absinthe knows that she is unable to divulge details, except to refer to aspects of her job that are described on the corporate website.

"*Beche de mer*," she says, referring to the sea cucumber fishery that is being poached to extinction by the illegal Chinese fishing boats that travel to every tropical reef in the world to take, and never give anything back.

Absinthe glances forlornly towards his bed. While he may have messed up the cleaning of the apartment, the preparation of his boudoir has been undertaken with some skill. Clean sheets, bees wax candles. A box of oils, scented and unscented. Lighting to suit any mood. The bed has an exotic quilt cover and fluffy but thin pillows. He looks up to see Turtledove looking at him. She shrugs her cheek as if to say, "Sorry to disappoint." And then she gets right down to the business of disappointing.

"I have really enjoyed our time together, Absinthe," she says honestly, and plainly. "The night that we spent sleeping under the truck was really very memorable. But my life is so hectic right now and will be for the foreseeable future. I really can't offer you anything. Do you understand?"

Absinthe's eyes fall to the floor, where he sees one of his socks. He shifts it with his foot under the table.

"And besides," Turtledove says, pepping up. "We have a communications challenge that needs problem-solving."

"I thought you were dead."

"I know." She slides her arm across the table and allows Absinthe to take her hand between his palms. Her hand is warm and soft and he strokes it, mesmerized by the sensation. She moves over to him, rises his face and kisses him on the mouth. She holds her face close to his and allows him to bask in the warm glow and the delightful scent of her mouth. "This is Turtledove proof alive. You have to let me go, Absinthe. You can't be talking to my director, like that. Do you understand?"

Absinthe nods his head gently, but that is a lie. He doesn't understand. He lacks the organ that allows one to understand these sorts of things. For him these things arc all a blur, a suite of concepts that he just can't quite grasp. It's like listening to a scientist talk about quantum physics, and you just go "*Uh-huh*" and "*Uh-hum*" as if you know what they are talking about, but in reality you got completely lost as soon as you were told that an electron is an elementary particle. The moment you are asked a question, you're fucked.

Turtledove resumes her seat and retrieves her hand. She raises her glass, "Cheers."

Absinthe fails to respond, instead stares at the breadcrumbs and margarine on the kitchen table.

Turtledove kicks his leg under the table. "Cheer up, soldier. I'm only here of a little while. Entertain me."

Absinthe comes out if his doldrums and beams a cheeky smile. "Do you like what I've done with the place?"

"The wee bucket and mop are a nice touch."

"I tried to clean the apartment, but I got distracted with the boudoir."

"Top marks for bedside manner. No marks for domesticity. That's you all over."

They both laugh, and it is nice.

"So what was the communications challenge?"

"Oh, yes. Thanks for reminding me." Turtledove retrieves her smartphone and goes to her messenger app. "I had to do a communications audit."

"On what?"

"On you, Rhinohorn."

"How did I go?" he asks, not wanting to hear the answer.

"This one here, text message, 'be careful', that was sweet. I liked that one. And then the next day, a cryptic one."

Absinthe feels like he is being analysed and it makes him uncomfortable. He knows that he's not well-made, and that he has all manner of malfunctions, some of which are fixable, others not. He knows that he is not well-suited to be with someone like Turtledove. There are big changes that he needs to make in his life so as to not routinely give her reasons to question her involvement with him. He knows what some of these are. As for the others, it's an agonising slow reveal. She's revealing some of them now.

"I you," Turtledove says, breaking him from his mind-miles. "That one's pretty harmless, I guess, because it doesn't really mean anything," She says this with a frosty, analytical tone.

Absinthe flattens. That was a deeply profound message that signified that he believed that he was in-tune with her, like an entangled photon. A change is required in the thinking around that, obviously.

Then she says, "Ah! Yes, this one. Sent 2am your time, post-wine. Your witching hour. This one arrived just as I was kicking off a Pangolin Unit briefing with the International Union for the Conservation of Nature. Or what's left of nature, anyway. This was in a conference hall in the Radisson Hotel in Hong Kong not so many hours ago. There were about sixty people in the room. The Chief Executive of the IUCN was seated right beside me, and I had foolishly – so, so foolishly – left my phone out because I was waiting for communication from the field."

Absinthe sighs, he knows where this is going.

"So here I am, briefing the IUCN on the valuable work that the Pangolin Unit does to prevent the sixth extinction of life on Earth, and along comes a message at a critical time. And what does it say? *I want you to suck my love you!* Really Absinthe!"

Absinthe mournfully looks down at the floor and sees the other sock. Oh, dear. This really isn't going so well, at all. He tries not to say anything inappropriate as Turtledove continues her debriefing on his communications audit.

"This is an official communication channel, Absinthe! These messages can be subpoenaed by a High Court and go on official government records. This is not how I want my career to be remembered. Do you understand?"

He nods forlornly, not knowing where to start to come back from this low point.

"You know Absinthe, every morning I wake up in the knowledge that I am probably going to fail. Fail in my quest to make a meaningful impact in preventing the extinction of Earth's wildlife. It's pretty audacious to even try, really, what with half of all wildlife wiped out in the past fifty years and the projections showing the rest are on their way out due to climate change and the actions of the unsustainable super-predators called humans. But try I do, anyway. We track down these criminal gangs and bring what firepower we can to bear on them. But we are in the Great Unravelling now, and every year, the climate change becomes more pronounced, making the traditional ways of sustenance harder for millions of poor people who can make a little money on the side capturing a pangolin here, a rare parrot there. Maybe some lemurs. Some seahorses. Maybe even knock of some megafauna if they are lucky, like a rhino, or a couple of hundred hippos. Absinthe?"

He looks up from the sock, with doleful eyes.

"I really didn't need that last message."

He nods with as much empathy as he can muster.

She takes his hand in hers and implores. "You are not a bad man, Absinthe. You are a good man. You are. And you didn't do anything wrong, really. I just I can't have this in my life, right now. Maybe in a different time it would be possible."

Absinthe looks up, hearing a change in her intonation. Maybe there is another option?

She continues, "Maybe in a time when the sixth extinction of life on Earth wasn't imminent; when the ocean wasn't on the verge of flipping into an anoxic state. Maybe if there wasn't 450 parts per million CO2 in the atmosphere and the Arctic hadn't tipped, almost overnight, to a hot phase. Maybe in that world, we could be together and have adventures like sleeping under trucks, and wading through mangrove mud with all those damned snakes. But not in this world. Not right now. It just can't be."

Turtledove stands. She leans forward and kisses the crown of his head. She raises his face to hers again and says the final words. "I have to be on a plane back to where the triads are. Don't be sad. I have only good memories of you."

And then she just leaves. She walks out the door in her overcoat with her handbag, and she's gone.

Save the Planet by Sundown

Absinthe wakes, filled with dread. It's not the dream that is still fresh in his mind that bedevils him, it's the feeling of certainty that something dark and grim has befallen his world. The dream was bizarre. In it he wakes to see a woman's clothes lying on his floor, like one would expect the morning after a wild night of debauchery, love, lust, intimacy and all that good stuff that humans do when they stop being so fucking corporate. What is a corporation, anyway, but a fictitious entity that can own and sue, but it can't kiss or love or fuck? Why would anyone choose that as a frame of reference, other than that they were overly acquisitive or litigious?

In his dream, there was a blue cocktail dress on the floor, black high-heels and knickers. That's all, and rightly so, as anything else would have been overdressed. But when Absinthe turned in his bed, in his dream, there was no woman there. And when he turned back to the studio apartment floor, all the woman's clothes were gone.

It is enough to make one question one's memory. Granted, he woke up without a girlfriend in his bed. But did he ever actually have a girlfriend in the first place? Was Turtledove just a tormenting dream?

Absinthe stumbles out of bed and stands in the middle of his studio apartment. He may as well be standing in the middle of a desert or drifting in space. Or drowning in the Canfield Ocean, the smell of rotten-egg gas his last experience of having lived on the fucked-up planet Earth. He feels an overwhelming sense of loss. It's as though a part of him has been cruelly excised during the night, and now he must get by without it, with no frame of reference about how to do this. On top of these anxieties is a hangover, and a dark thought, a question: did he send any inflammatory texts last night? He glances around for his phone and sees the phone body, the back cover, and the battery in three different locations on the floor. That's a sign of something. Did he dismantle the phone before or after the witching hour? And given that he is in the deepest, darkest hole, does it even matter? The good thing about rock-bottom is that it doesn't get any deeper without a jackhammer or one of those ground-penetrating bombs.

He stumbles into the bathroom where he sees a note-to-self scrawled on the mirror. It is written in lipstick, one of Turtledove's that he had found under his bed one day and forgot to return. The fuchsia ink reads a simple message: 'try not to'. That's called 'Absinthe succinct'. It's short, to the point, and widely open to interpretation.

"Try not to what?" he wonders. He answers his own question. Try not to further alienate Turtledove because there is still a chance. "A chance of what?" he wonders as he stands there swaying in front of the lipstick-smeared mirror. There's no chance of them being together while the biosphere is dying and abrupt climate change hangs over their heads like a sudden warming of the stratosphere. But maybe he can fix that? Right? That's got to be easier than fixing himself…

This thought – naïve, deluded, irrational and idiotic as it is – buoys him to crack a smile in front of the mirror. And seeing the smiling Rhinohorn fills him with enthusiasm for the day, and a general sense that he is not going to be hung, drawn and quartered just yet. He can work with that. All he has to do is save the planet by sundown. There's a mission worthy of one who is at the pointy end of Bitcrime Division. It's a big mission. A long journey. And a journey of a thousand miles begins by finding your socks. And Absinthe Rhinohorn knows exactly where his socks are. They are under the kitchen table.

Zips in the Wire

Maintaining that 'front of mirror smile' proves to be short-lived, and within the hour Absinthe's mood sours. He's driving his car to Dr Stent, the cardiologist, for the report on the malicious code in his pacemaker. It's during this journey that his fraught thoughts overwhelm the defences of his naïve optimism about seeing Turtledove again by saving the planet by sundown.

His smile slips as he pulls up at the traffic lights. At that point, he thinks back to the brooding sense of ill-ease that he woke with, and a picture forms in his mind. It is something to do with the elevator in the basement of the corporate offices. The last time he had thought of that place, he had observed a kind stranger, a first responder, attending to one of the victims of Absinthe's desire to live a life unencumbered by other people's intent.

The thought persists as he parks up in front of the cardiologist surgery. Zombie-like, he marches to the reception desk and announces his name. But his name is not required because the receptionist has been counting down the hours for his return. With her name badge positively bristling on her left breast, she says, "Hello, Mr Randy Horn." However, her amorous advance fails to provoke a reaction. Instead, he follows her instruction to sit, and the next conscious thought that he has is when he agrees to follow Dr Stent into his surgery.

"You look a bit vague, Absinthe. Is everything okay?"

"I don't have a girlfriend," he says, solemnly.

"Well, I am glad that's resolved. The last thing that you need right now is a distracting love interest."

"How so?" Absinthe is disarmed.

"I ran some tests on the code that I pulled out of your pacemaker. It seems your enemy is within."

"I don't understand. What does that mean?" Absinthe stammers.

"The soldiers call it 'Zips in the wire' I am led to believe. Anyway, the Internet of Things is very vulnerable to cyber-crime, Absinthe, as well you know. And your pacemaker is no less vulnerable than a printer or a refrigerator because they all contain a CPU and a modem. Everything on the internet of things is thus exposed to a whole world of computer-savvy criminals. This includes your toaster, your electric toothbrush, and your heart."

"What are you saying?"

Dr Stent leans close. "My investigation into the rogue code in your pacemaker lead me to you, Absinthe. Not you, exactly, but to a man named Horace, an operative of Bitcrime Division."

"Horace? I don't understand. What are you saying?"

"No names were mentioned, so there will be no difficult conversations when you go back to work, but it seems as though the pointy end of Bitcrime Division got made by the bad guys."

Absinthe stands abruptly, towering over the seated Dr Stent. He is about to utter an incomplete sentence when the Doctor waves him down again.

When Absinthe is seated again, Dr Stent explains clearly, "The crypto-miners, they got to your heart, Absinthe. The malicious code was the script for Love Coin. They've been mining a cryptocurrency called Love Coin on your pacemaker. That's why your heart rate has been so high. The faster they can make your heartbeat, the more money they make."

"The crypto-rats are mining me?" Absinthe stammers. "But you deleted the malicious code, right?"

"I removed it yesterday, Absinthe. But you are permanently wired into the Internet of Things. Everything is. And increasingly, everyone is. There are updates and data transfers going on all the time, mostly benign, but sometimes malicious. They've probably uploaded fresh code already, and they could be using your body as a cryptocurrency mining rig as we speak. How's your heart, Absinthe?"

"How's my heart? I've had enough of the damned thing! I want to tear it out. It's more trouble than it's worth right now." Absinthe is standing again, distraught.

Dr Stent waves him down once more. "Sit down soldier and listen to your doctor."

Absinthe sits, now conscious of the hammering of his heart. Some unidentified stranger is benefitting from his discomfort. How the tables will be turned when the pointy end of Bitcrime Division catches up with them. Absinthe thinks of the armoury in the basement of Bitcrime Division HQ. There are enough guns in there to raze the whole city. And bullets. Lots of fucking bullets.

"You need to channel that anger, Absinthe. Direct it towards your enemy, not towards yourself. It's not your fault, you see."

"Not? What's not my fault?"

"It's not your fault that your pacemaker got hacked. There are hundreds of people had their pacemakers hacked by Love Coin, so I have learned. And it's not your fault that your recent love affair has failed."

Absinthe is taken aback that he should be getting these insights from his heart doctor. At first he is perturbed by it, and then he softens. "How do you know that?"

"You are not well made, Absinthe. Whilst you may be perfectly formed to ventilate cryptocurrency miners, you are not well adapted for relationships with women. This doesn't mean you shouldn't try. On the contrary, you should keep trying. It's well worth it if you can find a good wife for a happy life. But for you, there will be struggles and misfires. Just be comfortable that you are still in the game. And think warmly of your recent love lost. You have learned much from her."

Then Dr Stent returns to the topic of the crypto-code on his pacemaker, but Absinthe isn't hearing him. Instead, he is falling down the rabbit hole of his own consciousness, bumping his head against every protruding tree root on the way down. He's not well made for relationships. He knows that, but had always felt that somehow it was the shortcomings in his character, that he was deliberately, yet unwittingly doing something wrong; that he 'was' to blame... But if the doctor is correct, and he's not to blame, then this is one bit of baggage he can set aside. His involvement with Turtledove was so highly unlikely in the first place that there's no shame that it should have imploded. Sure, sending a smutty, post-wine text message that mixed fellatio with love, and that got read by the Director of the IUCN didn't help the situation. But who was to know? Right?

Absinthe inhales deeply, feeling the oxygen flood his veins. He exhales at length, blowing out all the stress and angst that he had been carrying with him for days. He feels light-headed, and for the first time in ages, he is free.

He cracks a good-old Rhinohorn smile. He is, let's face it, named after an alcoholic beverage and an illicit aphrodisiac. Probably not such a bad idea to play to those strengths.

"I want you to suck my love you," Absinthe tells Dr Stent.

"I'm sorry," the cardiologist says, taken aback.

"That's my new motto."

"That's the spirit," Dr Stent slaps his shoulder, enthusiastically. "Now, until we can find a patch to keep those crypto-miners out of your heart, I ought really to keep you here under observation."

Absinthe stands, offers his hand. "Thank you, Doctor, I'll take it from here."

Back at the reception desk, Absinthe signs out and notices the receptionist grinning at him. "Did I see you at the Jungle Bar, the other day?" she asks.

"*Humm*? No, I don't go there. I drink at Bazooka Bar."

"Is that where they serve the nitro-glycerine cocktails?"

"Yeah. That's the place."

"Maybe I'll see you there, sometime?"

"Maybe," says Absinthe, absent-mindedly.

"I'm Marmalade," says the receptionist.

"I'm sorry?"

She proffers her left breast on which there is a name badge that confirms what she just said. It reads: Marmalade.

It's Not His Fault, Afterall

Driving his car away from the cardiac surgery, Absinthe feels light-hearted and philosophical. It is as though he has come through a wall of fire, unscathed. At least for the foreseeable future there is clarity, levity and the capacity to think of things objectively and not get all tangled up in the emotional elements. He sighs at length as he drives. He's thinking about Turtledove bouncing him out of her life. On one hand, it seems cruel and untoward, but that's him thinking like a self-centred single man. And let's face it, he doesn't really know what goes on in Turtledove's mind.

Sure she would tell him things, lecture him, actually, about how he ought to behave around her. On and on it would go, for hours, it would seem. It was like an unending list of alterations that needed to be made in order for her to tolerate his company.

"The posh one's like a bit of rough," that's what Horace had told him once, and Horace would know because he reads science papers. In fact, even Carly, the Rambo lesbian, had concurred that refined women often are attracted to men who were largely unsuitable, and all in the need for a bit of variety. That confirms it. No need to get Helmet's opinion on the matter.

Absinthe sighs. It's all too much for him to make sense of. At least for now he's not anxious or freaking out. Turtledove is safe, and really, in all honesty, she is probably better off without him. And if he were as concerned for her well-being as he claims to be, the best he can do is wish her well in whatever she does, where-ever she does it, and with whom. And so that's what Absinthe commits to do.

He pulls his car up at a set of lights and gazes wistfully into the distance. For the first time in a long time, he finds that he has nothing to do. All his key relationships are parked in a stable place. The Director thinks he's okay, to the extent that this is possible. His team have been put in their place for insubordination. And Turtledove is alive and well and where she chose to be, albeit without him. Sure, he's got some cryptocurrency mining rig hooked into his heart muscle, but Horace will sniff those miners out like a terrier on the trail of a rodent's nest. Those crypto-rats will be tagged and bagged in no time.

Absinthe sighs again, enjoying the feeling of freedom. The light turns green, and he drives, conscious of the fact that he doesn't know where he is going. Ah, yes. That's right. The elevator on the basement of the corporate offices. It's been playing on his mind all morning. He'd woken in quite a state thinking about that place. So, with nothing better to do, he turns his car in the direction of the corporate headquarters of the Department of Planetary Boundaries Defence, neither knowing nor particularly caring why.

The Turtledove Moment

There is a moment when it becomes clear that the 'calm' is actually the calm before the storm. There's no official name for this temporal juncture, so let's give it a name right now. Let's call it the 'Turtledove Moment' for the want of a better name. This is the instant in which you are jolted out of a sense of complacency and into a headspace of brooding anxiety. It's the moment in which you realise that maybe everything is not where it should be, after-all. That something is amiss.

In passing through the Turtledove Moment, the sensation is not overt. At first it is so subtle that it is barely noticeable at all. It's sort of like that realisation that the compressor on the refrigerator has stopped running, and then it gradually dawns on you that you don't actually have a refrigerator... The skin on your arm doesn't goose in an instant, but subtly grows until you look down, see the speckled flesh, and respond with a jolt of surprise.

The Turtledove Moment is imperceptible before-hand, and only barely perceptible a moment later. But a change, and a transition it most certainly is. It's the fourth domain of knowledge manifesting itself, the 'what you didn't know you knew all along' becoming known.

As Absinthe pulls his vehicle onto the down ramp of the underground carpark in the basement of the Department of Planetary Boundaries Defence he is still in the calm. As he fossicks around in the glove compartment for the tag, he is still in the calm. And as he swipes the tag across the reader he is as oblivious of the impending Turtledove Moment, almost as if it didn't exist in his immediate future. But exist it did.

The carpark boom rises, reminding Absinthe of a soldier's arm forming a salute. At the top of its arc, however, the soldier's hand doesn't hold there, motionless as it should.

Instead, the boom reverberates up and down, up and down, like it was made of rubber.

"Strange," thinks Absinthe, watching the metal pole bouncing around, where it ought really to have come to a brisk halt. It is at that exact time that the Turtledove Moment passes, and over the period of a few seconds, Absinthe begins to feel as if something were amiss in the world. It is subtle, at first, a sense not of ill-ease, but that comfort can't be taken for granted. His forearms rest on the steering wheel and he peers up through the windscreen at the boom gate that has finally stopped come to rest. And then it dawns on him. "What the hell am I doing here?"

The elevator, he thinks. It's something to do with the elevator. The sense of dread and foreboding returns. However, unlike this morning when this concept shredded him, now he is circumspect. Curious even. He has a steady hand and intends to investigate this perplexity with the demeanour of a man at ease. He pulls his car to park and steps calmly out of the vehicle. He walks three paces from the car, looks left and right, and then hits the wireless key, allowing the vehicle to Whoop! Whoop! behind him. He walks calmly towards the elevator, and when he arrives at the closed metal doors, he presses the 'up' button, as if he actually wanted to go up.

For a few moments, Absinthe has the privilege of observing his own fuzzy reflection in the metallic elevator doors. There's not much to be seen but a blur of colour that is distinct from the surroundings. Really, it could be anyone standing in front if the metal doors. And then the doors slide open, and Absinthe is staring at his own reflection in a perfectly mirrored surface. What he sees doesn't surprise him. He's a soldier, battle hardened, socially and emotionally inept, but otherwise making the best of the tools he was given. But there is something out of place. He wears a frown. A frown that suggests an unsolved mystery. What the hell is he doing here? Why does he feel as if a storm is about to break? He steps inside the elevator, towards his own perfect reflection, and in so doing he crosses a boundary and immediately feels the inadequacy that only a trained soldier can feel. It is summed up by a question, "Where's my gun?"

Absinthe turns, his heart racing. He is endangered and unarmed. For a moment he pauses, indecisive and then he steps out of the elevator. At that same moment, the black VW SUV pulls up sharply, right in front of him. This is the car that he saw Turtledove in, just a few days ago. The sight of the vehicle immobilizes him. The car is heading into the carpark, so the driver's side window faces him, now. Absinthe peers at the dark, tinted glass, unable to see who is inside. He hears the sound of the petrol engine running. It is revving fast and filling the air with vehicle exhaust. The sound of its engine syncs with the revving of his heart as the Love Coin crypto-miners exploit every pulse of that life-giving organ for their own personal gain.

Finally, after what seems an age of peering into the opaque glass of the driver's side door, the window descends a few inches, and Absinthe is able to see who is inside

He steps toward the car door and looks directly at Clarence Maidmont, Turtledove's boss, sitting in the driver's seat. She wears a fraught look as if she is grappling with difficult and challenging thoughts. Absinthe feels his heat rising as he waits for the Director to say something, but she remains mute, almost scared to open her mouth, as if the thing that she has to say might cause and explosion. With Absinthe impatiently breathing on her, she begins to tremble, and her hand moves to the electric window switch. The window rises and Absinthe grips the edge only to have his fingers trapped against the upper door frame. The pain increases, but rather than give in, Absinthe digs in and fights against the electric motor that threatens to sever his fingers. The struggle persists, and Absinthe grits his teeth, pulling down harder until there is the sound of the motor fizzing and sparking as it burns-out, the smell of ozone and burnt rubber, consistent with a fire in a crypto-mining rig. The window comes free and falls. Absinthe pokes his head into the cabin so that he is nose to nose with Director Maidmont.

"Turtledove?"

The Director both shakes and nods her head.

"Something happened?" Absinthe growls.

Clarence nods her head vigorously. "I have to go to work," she tells him, then promptly drives on.

The Chong Triad

There is an invisible line in some people that separates madness from sanity, and for Absinthe Rhinohorn, that line represents the very best decision-making space. Too mad, and stupid things happen. Too sane, and he becomes gripped with indecision as he plots out the consequences of every action. When he straddles that line, he is able to source the best from his rational thoughts and his intuition, as these two streams of thought synergize into excellent ideas.

Absinthe is that place now, sort of. At least, he is moving back and forth over that line as he swings between two states. In one moment, he has the clarity and the calm sanity of having had his heart doctor speak sage wisdoms. In the next moment, he suffers the intense dementia of a love-sick action-man.

As he rides upwards in the elevator. He emits a low frequency growling noise, the likes of which might be heard from a pack of circling timber wolves. He's got sparks of electricity flashing in all the various sections of his brain; through the medulla, the lizard section at the base, to the free-thinking part in the frontal cortex. Every piece of that ethanol-soaked organ is inflamed, fuelled by a torrent of simple thoughts: 'Directors must be punished', 'Is Turtledove alive?', 'Someone's going to pay' and 'Where's my gun?' He is so enraged that he doesn't even register how inappropriate it is to vault over the reception desk in the Biosphere Integrity unit, terrifying the poor young receptionist who cowers under the counter as he passes overhead. He storms through the busy office space, and parks himself inside the room that has the words 'Clarence Maidmont, Director' written on the door. He stands there emanating heat like a nuclear reactor, staring at the empty chair behind the desk.

Shortly, he has company. Two bruised security guards peer in through the door, their service revolvers drawn. "Don't move," one of the guards says. Then the guards are promptly dismissed as Director Maidmont shoos them away and moves behind her desk.

"Sit down, Absinthe. I have something difficult to tell you." She lays her phone on the desk face-up, waiting on communication from the field.

"What happened?" he asks, still standing.

"This is all unfolding as we speak. I can only tell you what I know and the facts may prove to be..."

"What happened!!?" bellows Absinthe Rhinohorn, his voice reverberating around the room like the percussion from a discharging artillery piece.

Director Maidmont tenses, suddenly fearing for her life. "No sooner had Turtledove returned to her Hong Kong office, than it came under attack."

"By?" Absinthe is rendered to single word sentences.

"Rocket propelled grenades."

"From?

"The Chong Triad."

"Turtledove?"

"Alive. Hospitalised. On her way back now. I think she's okay."

"Arriving?"

"She'll be touching down soon."

"Chong?"

"It's a Chinese criminal gang, heavily involved in wildlife trafficking. They are the subject of Turtledove's investigation."

"Eradicate," hisses Absinthe.

"We don't have the firepower. And it's too politically risky. We have to walk on eggshells just to stay in the country."

"I am firepower!" Absinthe growls.

"There is no way that your director would authorise an inter-departmental mission in a foreign nation."

"He has a need."

"And even if he did, it would need to get sign-off by the Chairman."

"Chairman?"

"Yes. The Chair of the Department of Planetary Boundaries Defence. And he can be a right effing asshole."

The Utility Bill

Minutes after departing Director Maidmont's office, Absinthe is back again. He holds out a sheet of paper and says, "My Director consents to my team problem-solving the Chong Triad if you can take care of this."

Director Maidmont takes the document and studies it. It is the invoice for the blown-up transformer.

"What's this?"

"Operational collateral damage."

"I see. So this is the price of having the pointy end of Bitcrime Division sort things out with the triad. Twelve point six million. That's a very expensive hit."

"Consider the cost of not hitting them, if they decide to come back," Absinthe responds quickly. "The Public Relations loss to your brand is worth $12.6 million alone. You might want to recoup that."

Director Maidmont glances up at Absinthe, unsure of where is clear-eyed corporate insight is coming from. In fact, Absinthe is just parroting what the Director of Bitcrime Division had told him to say moments before. It was one of those rare moments when Absinthe felt like he actually had a friend in the Director. The white-haired bureaucrat had even walked him to the door with his hand resting on Absinthe's shoulder. He had ended the brief conversation by saying, "It's so nice to have Absinthe Rhinohorn show up in the relationship. Pass my regards to Clarence."

"So, do you have a plan?" Director Maidmont asks.

"Yes. I am going to Hong Kong to shoot them."

"I mean do you have an operational plan?"

Absinthe hedges. No he doesn't because he hasn't tasked Horace with drawing it up, yet.

"Because for $12.6 million I expect the entire triad to be indefinitely annihilated. Not just the minions in the warehouse, I'm talking about the upper-echelon and everyone in between. If I am to commission Bitcrime Division as a mercenary force, I want that triad group permanently wiped from the face of this planet with maximum aggression to send a very powerful message that you do not mess with Biosphere Integrity. This is the platinum level service I'm buying here, Mr Rhinohorn." Director Maidmont waggles the utility invoice in the air. "I expect your operation to be flawless and completely covert. And I want to see lots of photos."

Absinthe nods solemnly, conscious of what he is getting himself into.

"So, you have until tomorrow afternoon to come up with an operational plan. Then you can it share with the Chairman."

"*Ahhh*, the Chairman," Absinthe says, glumly.

"Yes, the Chairman of the Department of Planetary Boundaries Defence. My boss. You didn't think that 'I' was going to seek his approval for this hare-brained scheme, did you?" Director Maidmont raises the utility invoice. "You get the Chairman's approval for this mission, I'll take care of your utility problem, and you can get revenge for what Chong Triad did to Turtledove."

Sleep-talking About George

After brokering a deal with the two directors to deliver righteous justice to several hundred unsuspecting Asians for their collective role in what happened to Turtledove, Absinthe finds his way to the hospital where she has been air-lifted. He waits anxiously at reception while the medical receptionist searches for Turtledove on their database and confirms that Absinthe is cleared to visit her. Permission to visit Turtledove in hospital was one of Absinthe's preconditions to Director Maidmont, who felt she had no reason to object, given that the lines between professional interest and personal had already been well and truly blurred.

Eventually, a nurse walks him to a private room and speaks quietly to him outside the door. "Your work college is fine. Okay? She's pretty shaken up from being so close to the explosion, but physically she's unhurt. She's sedated now, so try not to wake her. Just sit quietly."

"Thank you."

"And she sleep-talks."

"I'm sorry?"

"She talks in her sleep. She's been going on about some guy called George."

"George?" Absinthe is taken aback by the news. He knows about the sleep-talking. But George? Who the fuck is George?

The nurse pushes open the door to the dimly-lit room. Absinthe steps inside and stands at the end of the bed. He hears the door close behind him. Turtledove is asleep, as the nurse had said, and she is talking quietly. Absinthe moves to a chair and leans forward to be closer to her. She has her arms outside of the bedsheets, they are raised, and she gesticulates as she tells her story. Absinthe is familiar with this behaviour having been woken by her two or three times in the past. He'd thought it cute, another reason to dote over her.

"Oh, and that George, he does like a drink or two," Turtledove says, her eyes closed, her hands waving in the air.

"George?" thinks Absinthe, again. Who the hell is George? A dark thought flickers through his mind like a thin, fleeting strike of lightning, but it quickly fades. He wants what's best for her, where-ever and with whom-ever she is, that's his commitment. Right?

"And when George comes in, he's got that smell about him."

"Smell?" thinks Absinthe. Is she referring to a cologne?

"I do like that George, and I know that he's crazy about me. George will sort things out."

Absinthe feels his heart sink, and he wonders whether he really ought to be sitting there tuning into Turtledove's thoughts, uninvited. And besides, the last thing he wants to do is to hear the details of her affections for another man. The very concept that there is another man makes Absinthe's stomach cramp and his heart surge. Those Love Coin miners will be making a fortune from him today!

Sitting there, learning of Turtledove's other life is gruelling for Absinthe, but he is unable to tear himself away. And yet, staying, being so close to the woman with whom he has been intimate, and for whom he is still emotionally attached; to hear her muttering in her sleep about fucking Georgey-boy, makes him feel like he has allowed himself to be led meekly to a knackers yard where he is the surprise guest of a gelding ceremony. Rendered emasculate. A cuckold. It's not a thought that sits well with him, and he starts to fidget with anxiety.

Absinthe goes to move, but he is struck by Turtledove's new sleepy statement. "And when there is a mess like this, no other man is as capable is as George. Just no one. Only George."

Absinthe stands, his doleful eyes unable rise above the floor. He exits the room feeling hollow and alone.

Outside, in the corridor, he draws his hand down his face feeling wretched and inadequate. He glances around for something, anything to distract him or change his frame. He sees a bucket with mop sticking out of it parked in the hallway, just sitting there like it were in his own lounge room, a testament to his own inept domesticity.

Absinthe is reminded of just how ridiculous he has become; unable to even clean an apartment. He has been pursuing a woman with all of his heart, and with not the emotional maturity to properly read the signals. Any of them. Boy, that George character got a free kick when Absinthe sent the smutty text message, he thinks. He lets out a long sigh, feeling as thought the only thing that he wants to do is to start drinking, to numb the sensation of being a human being with an inadequate grasp of his own feelings.

Mournfully, he walks slowly along the corridor, knowing that he has some intensive work stuff to do before he can start numbing himself out. Somehow, he has to convince his team to join him on a mad-cap, hyper-dangerous mission that he is now uncertain that he wants to go through with, himself.

Balls in the Air

As it happens, Horace gets quite excited about the mission to knock off the Chong Triad and commits to having an operational plan by midday the next day, allowing Absinthe plenty of time to absorb the plan before pitching it to the Chairman of the Department of Planetary Boundaries Defence.

Clearly, Horace is not the problem. The problem is Helmet and Carly who are still sore at him for having machined-gunned the tunnel close to their heads.

"And fuck me, if I haven't still got concrete dust in the back of my throat," Helmet grumbles, reinforcing the sentiment by making hacking noises, attempting to regurgitate concrete dust, to prove his point. Absinthe reacts, recognising this as the sort of bad behaviour that would make Turtledove squirm and pull away. He's woke to that sort of behaviour now, and intolerant of it.

"I get it, Helmet. You don't have to embarrass yourself."

"Embarrass? What? I was just coughing."

"What's going on with you, Absinthe?" Carly asks, annoyed. "You've gone all pussy-foot around Bitcrime Division. We go in boots first, dude, remember?"

"It's time to raise our standards," Absinthe grumbles. "We are going international and undercover. Put your game face on."

"So, Helmet can't have a little cough without you getting your panties in twist," Carly protests. "Anyway, I've applied for a job on Mars, so I probably won't be around this Mickey Mouse outfit for too much longer."

"Well, until you go to Mars, you work for me," Absinthe snaps, authoritatively. "So keep you shit wired tightly. We're going full-Rambo on a bad-ass triad right soon."

Absinthe suddenly feels like the balls in his pants have been replaced by balls in the air. He's lost count of how many balls he has now. Normally, he just goes along with Horace's plan, shoots anything that moves, then reports to the director. That's changed. Now, he's got all the regular work pressures; his turbulent feelings about Turtledove; the expectations of the two Directors; the thought that Turtledove has bounced him out of her life; an international, undercover murder-mission to execute flawlessly; the thought that Turtledove has this bizarre George fellow sniffing around her; having to deal with two bitching and whining team members: Carly, soon to go to Mars, apparently, and Helmet, soon to get smack if he doesn't wise up; an imminent meeting with the Chairman of the entire fucking Department of Planetary Boundaries Defence; and then there is Turtledove, ever-present in his thoughts. It's exhausting. It's totally exhausting trying to keep up. Guns, bullets, and ethyl-alcohol are so much easier.

Plus, he thinks, all of the above are all tied up with his obsession with Turtledove. And question. At what point did his life bifurcate, and he chose to take the road less travelled. Yes, good question. When did this madness start? It wasn't the first time he laid eyes on Turtledove, nor the second, nor the third. That was infatuation at first, second and third sight; that's benign. No harm ever comes from that. No, the bifurcation happened the moment that he approached her at the buffet. He went to speak, totally clammed up, and had become an inadequate force from that moment on; an ordinary man seeking to impress upon an extra-ordinary woman. How was that ever going to end up in anything other than a train wreck, with him munched up in the twisted debris, and her, unharmed, looking in, wondering why anyone would do that to themselves?

Absinthe sighs, forlornly. He doesn't want to get drunk. He just wants to be unconscious until everything is forgotten. How long would that take? A month? A year? But that's all wishful thinking. Right now the task at hand is to gain the complicity of Helmet and Carly for his mad mission. Horace sweeps into the rescue.

"Fuck me, look at this bullshit," he grumbles, turning his computer around to show off a series of images on the screen. "These triad rats are shooting tigers. Fucking tigers, man!"

"You have to be shitting me," Carly pours over the computer like she was personally affronted by the news. She flicks through the images, aghast.

"I shit you not," Horace replies. "What have we been doing ventilating crypto-miners when we could have been knocking-off wildlife poachers? I want a transfer."

"What do I know about shooting tiger poachers?" moans Helmet.

"It's just like shooting a crypto-rat," Absinthe advises, sagely. "Just aim for the centre of body-mass and squeeze the trigger."

He wonders why he is even having this conversation. Normally, he'd just call an order and his team would comply. He reverts to his old routine: brisk demands. "Okay, mofos. We're bouncing into action in 36 hours. Be ready!"

He departs the building, craving to be in his own space, his heart hammering, and desperately hoping that he has a team to accompany him to take on the Chong Triad when it is time to bounce out in 36 hours' time.

The Green Fairy

As promised, Horace comes through with an operational plan to liquidate the entire Chong Triad in short order. The plan is Horace-excellent, concise, and well thought-through. Horace had spent the night on the phone to various intelligence agencies, and on-ground, in-country assets. The British intelligence agency GCHQ had a full dossier on the triad and were more than happy at the idea of an outside force bringing fire to bear on them.

Horace briefs Absinthe on the plan at midday, and he is immediately impressed. It is a short, sharp, maximum aggression, platinum-level, hyper-drone, ultra-kill-box, fuel-air-explosive, and a just kilo-tonne of TNT short of tactical nuke. It is exactly the sort of plan that you'd need if you wanted to send a resounding signal to the world that you shouldn't fuck with Biosphere Integrity.

Horace's operational plan to liquidate Chong Triad puts Absinthe in a mood sound enough to go to the Chairman of the Department of Planetary Boundaries Defence and try to convince that he should be allowed to execute it.

"It's a good plan," he reassures himself as he waits in the cold corridor outside the huge wooden door, beyond which is the safe operating space of the much-dreaded Chairman. Absinthe stands in a stone tunnel, much like the catacombs of an old church. It is still and quiet with just the faint and distant sound of dripping water. He has butterfly the size of fruit bats flapping in his stomach. It's like there's a whole flock of them in there, squabbling over food.

His heart is churning, pumping way too much blood. Meanwhile, his pacemaker sparks away, sending electrical pulses to the pump muscle, and at the same time calculating the cryptographic hashes required to mine Love Coin, and verify transactions on the blockchain.

Absinthe lets out a long sigh as he remembers Turtledove sleep-talking about that fucking asshole, George. Jeez, he'd like to go toe-to-toe with that George character. And then he thinks that that is exactly the sort of macho-bullshit that would be off-putting to Turtledove. Best he let that idea go and come up with a more inspiring interpretation of the facts.

"Maybe George is Turtledove's uncle?" Absinthe thinks. Uncle George, maybe. He ponders that for a while, and during that time, he forgets to be angry.

Just then, the hinges on the big wooden door start to creak, the door opens part-way, and a man who has a striking resemblance to a tall, ugly monk comes into view. He steps into the hallway, glances left and right as if to check that they were alone, and then looks Absinthe up and down as if her were appraising him as a component of a ceremonial feast. Satisfied that Absinthe is edible, and with a slow drawling voice, the monk-man says, "State your name and the purpose of your visit."

"My name is Absinthe Rhinohorn. I am here to speak with the Director of the Department of Planetary Boundaries Defence about a secret mission to annihilate Chong Triad."

"Absinthe? Like the green booze?" Monk-man asks with a disapproving tone.

"Yes."

"Rhinohorn? Like the libido enhancer?"

"That's correct."

"You had best follow me." Monk-man steps inside the big wooden door and when Absinthe enters, he pushes the door closed, forcing the dry hinge to squeak again.

Absinthe follows the strange man along another stone passageway, and they come to another door beyond which is a huge chamber, like the inside of a cathedral. It is dimly lit inside this vast room, but a beam of sunlight shines down through coloured glass, illuminating a patch of stone. Monk-man has Absinthe stand on a particular flagstone. In this position, the beam of light shines in his face. He raises his forearm to block out the sunlight, so that he can make out a figure, a person, interrupting the beam. Monk-man walks away, and Absinthe hears the door squeak closed behind him.

The person in the beam of light is high up, and far away, and Absinthe adjusts his arm to see as best as he can. The Chairman is barely discernible, what with the light beaming down all around him. However, his voice is exceptionally clear, reverberating off the stone walls and focussing on the very place where Absinthe's head is.

"So, you are the man called Absinthe Rhinohorn," the Chairman begins.

"Yes, Sir."

"Speak up man, I can't hear you."

"I said Yes Sir, Sir!"

"Sir, Sir? Tell me something Mr Rhinohorn. Do you believe that having been named after a spirit, the Green Fairy, has had any bearing on the way that your life turned out?"

Absinthe shuffles in his place unable to form a sensible answer. He's not even sure what the question means.

"And don't think to lie to me either, Mr Rhinohorn. I can see into your heart."

"I sometimes feel as though I am not in control of my own life!" Absinthe projects his voice towards the light.

"Relax man. None of us really are. How do you think we got into this mess?"

"Mess, Sir?!"

"The collapse of the biosphere. Let me share the story with you so that we are both on the same page."

"Very well, Sir!"

"It was a Northern winter in the early 2020s when an important climactic tipping point was crossed. A sudden stratospheric warming obliterated the jet streams that make up the Polar Vortex, allowing warm, moist air into the dark Arctic. When the sun finally rose, later in the year, all the ice was gone. And because the ice was no longer there, the Arctic warmed even more. And with the temperature differential between the Arctic and the Equator reduced, the driving force of the world's climate system slipped into history, unleashing the freak and intense weather events that characterised the Great Unravelling. It's been going on for years now; the *'The Great Unravelling of Centuries of Human Progress'*. For hundreds of millions of people this is a terrifying catastrophe, but for some, an opportunity for overdue change. Others and I called together the more enlightened Governments of the world and compelled them to get serious about protecting the Planetary Boundaries. They used Quantitative Easing to provide the necessary financial capital, and they agreed to the heavy-handed response to environmental crime that you yourself deliver with such proficiency. There is still no guarantee that the Great Unravelling will ever stop; we may simply be sliding to imminent human extinction. But it's still nice to get a little payback, don't you think?"

Absinthe nods, unsure what to make of it all. He's not so sure why he has been told that story and he wonders what comes next.

"Anyway, Mr Rhinohorn," the silhouetted Chairman says. "You didn't come here for a history lesson. What did you come here for? And more interestingly why am I talking to you and not your director?"

"I represent two Director's, Sir. I am requesting permission for an inter-departmental, international, undercover hit mission to destroy a triad that recently attacked operatives from Pangolin Unit, killing five of our people."

"Do you have a personal interest?"

"Sir?"

"What is your personal interest in this mission?"

"My friend was hospitalised," mumbles Absinthe.

"Speak up man! I may be sitting up here, God-like, but I can assure you that I have the hearing of a middle-aged man."

"My friend was hospitalised!"

"So you come here, because you want to get revenge for your friend?"

Absinthe looks at the floor. He feels as though failure has come quick.

"I'll give you some advice in answering that question. Think of the Venn Diagram."

"Sir?"

"The two circles. Do they overlap? One circle is your personal, selfish interest. And the other circle is the needs of these two departments you represent. Is there any overlap?"

"Yes, Sir."

"Describe it to me."

"Sir, I would like to take a team of four people, undercover, and eradicate the wildlife traffickers in the Chong Triad – all of them, from the minions in the warehouse to the three brothers at the top. I believe that is necessary to send a powerful signal that one should not mess with Biosphere Integrity."

"And being a triad there will be a lot of senior government and business elites feeding from the same trough. You going to shoot them too, Mr Rhinohorn? And this triad has hundreds of members. You going to shoot all of them?"

"I…," begins Absinthe, but he is not quick enough to keep up with the questions.

"And who is looking after the Public Relations, so that we can convince the important people to think what we want them to think, instead of them thinking for themselves?"

"I…,"

"And whose head is going to roll if the operation goes tits-up and the senior people in this organisation have to answer for operational collateral damage. Not to mention the violation of another nation's sovereignty. And who's going to pay to bail your team out of jail should they be caught?

"I…"

"You come in here with this half-baked plan, and you expect me to approve it, just like that?"

Absinthe flattens. His eyes fall to the floor.

"Well approved it is!" the Chairman's voice booms out across the cathedral-like space, almost as if God had said it, himself.

Absinthe looks up, stunned. Did he hear that right?

"Now, get out there Absinthe Rhinohorn and do to those wildlife traffickers what they do to the tiger, the pangolin and the *beche de mer*. Go and deliver some much overdue natural justice for the millions of species who have been sent to oblivion by the unsustainable super-predator *Homo sapien*. Some-one ought to pay. Go with my full blessing, you brave and committed man! And if it completely fucks up, as well it might, I'll guess we'll just have to sort something out. Go now!"

Stunned at his new fortune, Absinthe stumbles out of the beam of light. He takes a few moments for his eyes to adjust to the gloom. In this time the Chairman completes.

"And Mr Rhinohorn?"

"Yes, Sir."

"The way that we perceive ourselves is integral to the way that we behave."

"Yes, Sir."

"Your first name may be that of an alcoholic beverage. But did you know that one of the main uses of Rhino Horn in Vietnamese culture, is that of an anti-hangover tonic?"

"Really, Sir? I didn't know that."

"I think that given the intense nature of the job that you do, you are a remarkably balanced man. Thank you for giving me the opportunity to meet you. Good luck to you in your noble mission. Does it have a name, by the way?"

"A name, Sir?"

"The name of your mission."

Good question. Horace's briefing paper was simply titled 'Chong Triad, Hong Kong.'

"It's called Operation Turtledove, Sir," says Absinthe Rhinohorn.

Pong!

The next morning, on the plane to Hong Kong, Absinthe feels so totally out of his comfort zone. Horace's plan has them travel as civilians, and to team up with in-country assets who bring all the firepower, vehicles, and local knowledge. The pointy end of Bitcrime Division does the shooting, aided by the others, and if anything goes wrong, the local assets scram and leave Absinthe and his team to sort out the mess, themselves. It's tough love, no doubt, but often it's the only way to get a job done quickly.

Sitting on the commercial flight, dressed in civvies, and with not a gun in sight, Absinthe feels vulnerable and alone. He's also wholly sober and un-hungover, as he had spent the previous evening's drinking time staring at the unopened bottle. For hours he had sat there, his mind caught in a loop with a few elements: Turtledove is seeing a man called George - the Chairman thinks that he is balanced – he's going into combat tomorrow - he had embarrassed Turtledove with his smutty text message and lost her as a result - he has to stay sharp - he wants to kill George, but he has a self-imposed prohibition on thinking these thoughts. Over and over, the sequence of thoughts loop and loop until he drifted off to sleep, sitting upright at the kitchen table

Now, Absinthe feels so very sad, trapped there thinking about Turtledove, in the middle seat of the airliner with a stranger on either side. It's been so long since he met a girl that he liked, and one who liked him back. And now she's gone, as a result of his own foolish actions.

It's like having waited forever in a long queue, that when he finally got to the front, he realised that he had forgotten his paperwork, and had to leave the queue to retrieve the papers, only to join the queue at the far end. It seems like so little time had passed between being at the front and end at the end. It's like climbing up a muddy hillside all afternoon only to lose your foothold at the summit and slip back to the bottom again in seconds.

Absinthe's thoughts turn gloomier as the flight proceeds. He thinks that the collapse of the Turtledove relationship is a portend that no matter how long he waits in the queue, or climbs the slippery slope, he is always going to 'I want you to suck my love you it up' in the end. That he will be forever alone, at the back of the queue, at the bottom of the hill, covered in mud. He will have fleeting glimpses of the summit, be periodically smitten, then lovesick and alone again. Maybe that is how it will always be with him. Let's face it, that's kind of how it always had been in the past. So what has changed? Turtledove. That's what's changed. She impinged upon him in a way no other woman ever had. She scintillated and inspired him. She made him want to climb to the top of his own mountains and jump up in the air at the top. Poor Absinthe, a man with an overdeveloped capacity for action, but an underdeveloped emotional core.

It's as if he is some wind-up toy – like a little tin soldier powered by a spring set loose on a table-top. For a brief while, he marches across the table and stomps around, entertainingly. But then he promptly turns, marches at full speed towards the edge, and topples over. It's as if the fall is inevitable, as though his future is entirely predicted by the engineered elements that comprise him; the size of the cogs, the length of the spring, the structure of his mechanical parts. That no matter how many times the toy is wound-up and set free, it will always enjoy a brief period in which it performs adequately, and then – as if it were directed by a mean-spirited, intervening deity – the toy would inevitably careen to, and over, the table's edge. Over and over, the wind-up Absinthe would toss itself onto the hard floor, like a lemming, looping on Groundhog Day, until eventually, the repetitious force of impacting the ground, shook something loose, and it was Game-Over Absinthe Rhinohorn.

Absinthe is distracted from his thoughts by a distinctive aircraft noise. It is the 'Pong!' sound indicating that they are at cruising altitude, and it is safe to take off seatbelts. He sighs forlornly, feeling exhausted from all the thoughts, and realising the flight has only just begun, and he has hours more yet, stuck inside the miasmatical anxieties inside the dark well of his own mind.

Captain Nutcracker

Headquarters for Operation Turtledove is an old tuna boat tied up in a busy part of Hong Kong harbour. It's a big ship, old, iron, painted black, and with long streaks of rust on the hull. It is a fitting vessel upon which to plan a hit on wildlife traffickers, as this ship had participated in no small amount of ecocide, itself. For decades this shameful vessel had steamed the oceans hoovering up entire schools of fish, and all the things that accompany them, including dolphins, whale sharks, and turtles.

Below decks, there is a large room painted pale-grey with incandescent lamps glowing overhead. In this steel room, there are crates of machine-guns, rocket launchers and bazookas, enough munitions to start a decent sized war. On a central table, there are maps, charts, printed schematics and other mission critical documents.

Absinthe and his team huddle around the table and discuss the mission with the on-ground assets. These guys are from a private security contracting firm call Storm Front, and their bill is being paid by British GCHQ. There's five of them and they are led by a gnarly old Special Boat Service Major who goes by the name of Captain Nutcracker. He wears an eye-patch and excels in talking like a pirate with a thick Welsh accent. He's partial to saying things like: "I hope ye rum barrels are over-proof, and ye have a tight plug in ye bung-hole."

There are three target buildings in the operation, indicated on the map with a big red 'X' marked in three locations. The first is a warehouse complex which is used as a transhipment point for all manner of trafficked wild-life products. Given that there is no living wildlife in this complex - and the only living things are bad-guys - this part of the operation is a kill-box or a free-fire zone: if it moves, it gets ventilated. The second compound is where the triad tranships live animals.

To prevent endangered species becoming collateral damage, this place has much stricter rules of engagement. The plan is to flush the traffickers out of the building and have Helmet pick them off with a semi-automatic sniper rifle. There is some discussion about how to flush out the bad-guys without panicking the wildlife and this is resolved by a suggestion from one of the Storm Front team, a former Rhodesian army soldier called Larry. The third building is the residence of the Chong brothers who are the primary beneficiaries of all the suffering wildlife and the species tumbling into permanent extinction. There are photos of the brothers on the table, they are over-fed, short black hair, Kim Jong Un-types. Horace has named them Tweedle-dum, Tweedle-dee, and Tweedle-didn't. They inhabit a multi-storey, luxury apartment complex in an upmarket district unaccustomed to the sound of heavy machine-gun fire. Storm Front have confirmed that the brothers will be there and have a plan for how to ensure that women and children have left the building before the pointy end of Bitcrime Division pays a visit. However, they have yet to decide on how to knock off the brothers and their cronies.

"Leave that to me and Horace," Absinthe instructs the assembled team. With the debrief over, the nine mercenaries select weapons, and after that, retire to various parts of the ship to rest, recreate, drink, and ultimately sleep. Action starts at 5am the following morning.

Terminate With Extreme Prejudice

The attack on the warehouse full of animal products goes flawlessly. Absinthe and his three team members blast a hole in the roof and abseil into the gloomy, malodorous space, with guns blazing. The triad members are caught by surprise, and even though they are armed, to a man, they are unable to match the training or aggression that the pointy end of Bitcrime Division bring to bear. Terminate with extreme prejudice is, after all, not just a euphemism. A wall of fire descends on the mean-spirited wildlife traffickers; and within minutes, the triad gang has been routed, their ventilated bodies slumped over sacks of pangolin scales, twisted up in a stack of elephant horns, or blasted into chunks over crates filled with dried shark fin, or the component parts of tigers and other endangered big cats. Phase 1: Mission Accomplished.

In no time, Absinthe and his team is whisked away from all the remains of formerly living things and onto the next venue. In this place, there are precious endangered species kept alive. There is a cage full of ring-tailed lemurs smuggle out of Madagascar and destined to become pets for rich people in Russia and the Middle East. There is a box packed with sulphur crested cockatoos shoved inside coke bottles that have had their bottoms removed. Most are still alive, just, but some have perished from the maltreatment. In this warehouse there are also baby giraffes destined for private zoos. Tiger cubs. Owls. Exotic lizards, and even a sloth. None are being properly cared for. The cost to acquire them is so cheap, and the value of selling them so high that even if you lose half in transit, there is still pots of money to be made. In this warehouse complex, the pointy end of Bitcrime Division arrives not with a crash, but with a whisper. Three of the team suddenly appear inside the warehouse, purposely marching forwards. Their weapons, held at waist level, are set to semi-automatic - one bullet per trigger pull. The guns are fixed with silencers and loaded with slow, hollow-point rounds to minimise ricochet. The team march in, silently executing, throwing the dozens of triad workers into a panic. In terror, they stream out of the building, only to get cut down by Helmet's rapid sniper fire. A few of the poachers think to hide in the cages, and in so doing, they accidentally set free the captured wildlife. The warehouse is suddenly filled with running giraffe, tigers and cockatoos screeching overhead. "Watch out for the baby elephant!" shouts Horace to Absinthe, as the large-eared animal runs around the warehouse, trumpeting, excited to be free. It is pandemonium in there.

Once the traffickers of Phase 2 are fully ventilated, Absinthe and Horace depart for Phase 3 - the Chong brothers. Absinthe and Horace had visited the apartment block early that morning and set up a little surprise. Now, back in place on a rooftop overlooking the twelve-storey building, Absinthe and Horace watch as the women and children depart the building as per the cunning plan devised by Storm Front. Then the call comes that the building is empty save for the three brothers, their private security detail and various other senior members of the group.

"We're good to go," says Absinthe.

Horace retrieves the detonator and passes it over. The detonator sends a wireless signal to the shaped charges that they had placed in the pillars in the carpark under the building.

"So what's it all about, this mission?" Horace asks cryptically. "I mean it's a good mission. But one minute we're whacking crypto-miners, then overnight an international, interdepartmental mission for wildlife. Is there something else going-on that I ought to know about?"

Absinthe looks down at the detonator in his hand. It's a small box with a big red button and a switch to arm the device. He flicks the switch. Device armed. He looks over at Horace and thinks it through. On one hand, he is dying to tell the story about Turtledove, so that he can say her name and relieve himself of the burden of being the only person in the team to understand his motivations. On the other hand, it is none of Horace's business. And if he told Horace, what is to say that Horace wouldn't tell Carly and Helmet. Then they would all know that Absinthe had been putting his team at elevated risk, for personal reasons. That wouldn't do.

"Would you like to do the honours?" Absinthe asks, holding out the detonator.

"Why, thank you Sir." Horace reaches out, places his finger on the red button. He says theatrically, "Fire in the hole." They both snigger, Horace presses, and the explosives go off.

A cloud of dust erupts from the entrance to the carpark. The whole building seems to quiver and after a few moments, there is the sound of the explosion. The next thing that happens is that the entire building seems to drop about ten feet, as the pillars that hold the building up, give way. Then that sudden jolt stresses the pillars and walls that hold up each successive floor. The first floor collapses onto the ground floor, and the second floor collapses onto the first. And so it goes, all the way up to the twelfth floor. Crunch, crunch, crunch, crunch, crunch; twelve times until the building is a quarter of its height, and every one of the Chong Triad inside are squished into a paste between sheets of concrete.

"Whoa. That was awesome," Horace says, impressed.

"Pretty cool, huh?" Absinthe replies. "So what were you saying?"

"I don't know Absinthe. You've got some side operation running. I can always tell. I'm just interested to know what it is."

Absinthe nods at length, thinking it through. He says, "When we get back, I want you to turn your attention to Love Coin. You heard about that one?

"I got a call about it the other day. There's a lot of it about, but it don't concern us."

"Why not?"

"Because they aren't mining with mains electricity. They're using the energy from the heart. There's no carbon footprint."

"So, Horace."

"Yes, Boss."

"Do it anyway."

Frigging in the Rigging

Back on the ship after a hard day's murder, the combined forces of Bitcrime Division and Storm Front Security crack open a few cold beers and relax. Down below decks, in the room full of guns, they slip into varying stages of inebriation. Horace repeats at least five times the manner in which the twelve-storey apartment came down like a concertina, and then just stood there, a third of its original height. He slaps Absinthe on his shoulder playfully and old Rhinohorn even cracks one of his Rhinohorn smiles. This puts everyone in good cheer. Even Captain Nutcracker gets into action. He starts dancing the hornpipe and singing a song of his own making to the tune of Frigging in the Rigging:

- We took-out the Chong Triad

- For wildlife crime they were bad

- With bullets and guns

- We murdered some

- And squished them under concrete pad

Shortly, an officious-looking man from GCHQ visits, and the soldiers stop singing while he delivers four pieces of operationally important news. First, their battle damage assessment indicates that the Chong Triad is most definitely smashed beyond repair; second, that the few remaining members of the gang were being either picked up or picked off by the security forces, what he referred to as a mopping-up exercise; third, that the media had been alerted that a shadowy new rival group had been responsible for the hit, and that that was now the official version of events; fourth, that by all measures, the mission was successful, and that he foresaw no trouble with the Bitcrime Division exfiltrating the country, the next morning. His final action is to shake everyone's hand, thank them on behalf of the British Government, and leave behind a crate of French champagne.

Well, you can imagine how rowdy the party got from that point on! Drinking champagne from the neck of the bottle, the team descends to another level of inebriation. Carly and Helmet wrestle on the floor until they get hurt and decide to do something else. Horace tells everyone his theory about Abrupt Climate Change, but he's so smashed that he slurs his words, and no one knows what the hell is talking about. Absinthe and Captain Nutcracker engage in an arm-wrestling competition that goes on for so long, and is so exhausting, that they both fall asleep on the job.

An Invitation

Back home, Absinthe presents himself to his director and is pleasantly surprised with the old bureaucrat's demeanour. Absinthe is even offered to sit down, have a coffee and to share in detail the sequence of events. The Director "*Ummms*" and "*Ahhhs*" at each salient or operational aspect of Absinthe's tale.

"What sort of charge did you use to penetrate the roof?" he interjects, suddenly fascinated by Absinthe's life. "What was the average number of bullet holes in each body?" and "How many grams of plastic explosive did you use in the shaped charges to get that effect with the building?" As he is asking these questions, he is flipping through the photos taken by Storm Front Security showing the results of the battle: the blasted triad members, the rescued wildlife, and the pancaked apartment block.

When he is finally sated, the Director escorts Absinthe to the door with his hand on his shoulder and shares his new vision for the Bitcrime Division to branch out into other operational areas. "Maybe we can make these international forays a regular thing," he says.

On the next floor down, Director Maidmont is equally pleased to see him, and welcomes him with a hug. A hug!

"Well, I certainly did get the platinum level service," she says once Absinthe has walked her through all the grim photos and the operational aspects of the mission. "Triad?" she chuckles. "What Triad? Now, I dare say that you are eager to share the news of your victory with Turtledove."

"Is she well?" asks Absinthe, suddenly anxious.

"She's fine, just resting. Oh, and I nearly forgot. This is for you." Director Maidmont retrieves a white envelope upon which is written his name. "I had a peculiar conversation with the Chairman, the other night. It seems that you have friends in high places. He asked me to get this to you."

"What is it?" Absinthe asks, taking the envelope.

"It's an invitation to a corporate function for Department of Planetary Boundaries Defence Governors. And mercenaries, too, it seems. It is an excellent opportunity for you to either advance your career or destroy it completely."

"I don't understand."

"Talk to Turtledove. She'll explain. "You might even bring her along as your plus-one."

"Do you think she'll come?' Absinthe is suddenly alert to an exciting opportunity: going on a date with Turtledove.

"If she's feeling up to it, I dare say that she'd consider it.

George of the Jungle

Outside the door of Turtledove's hospital room, Absinthe halts, suddenly overwhelmed by anxiety. The drumming of his heart is almost audible, and he suddenly feels great doubt about going through with his plan. What if he goes into the room and George is there? What if there's a fight? That paralyses him, and he finds himself staring at the floor with the thought of another man with Turtledove turning over in his mind.

"Maybe I should go," he murmurs.

Then, almost as if she were listening in on his fraught thoughts, Turtledove is right there. She's wearing a stylish hospital gown and slippers, holding a bunch of flowers, and walking towards him. She's in high spirits and asks him directly, "George of the Jungle, did you wash that gunpowder smell out of your hair, and pick your wee socks up?" She gives him a brief hug, the sort of hug a friend would give to an ex-lover, when the friend wanted the ex-lover not to get the wrong idea.

"What?" is all that Absinthe is able to muster by way of speech.

"Have you come to pay a wee visit?"

"George? Who is George?"

"You are George."

"I'm George?"

"George of the Jungle. Socks on the floor." Then she starts to taunt him a contrived voice, "Deep in the crypto-mines lives a mysterious figure. His name is legendary. His strength is remarkable."

"I'm George."

"George'll fix it. As long as it needs shooting that is. Lol."

"George of the Jungle?" Absinthe is taken aback. It all makes sense now. That's her nickname for him, she'd used in numerous times, once when she found a used tea bag on the floor of his apartment. And another time when she sniffed his scalp and scolded him for bringing the smells of work home. "Gunpowder, brick-dust and blood," she called it.

She pushes the door open, arranges the flowers in a vase. Then she gets into bed, covers herself up.

"I'm having a wee relax," she tells him. "On doctor's orders." She pats the side of the bed and says, "Sit down Absinthe. Tell me what's going on. Did something happen in Hong Kong to the Chong Triad?"

Absinthe tells her, "The Chong Triad are no more."

Turtledove glances over to confirm that the door is closed. She lowers her voice. "Did you have something to do with that?"

"I am firepower," he tells her gravely.

"I assume that means yes."

"I asked the Chairman, and he gave it the go-ahead."

"The Chairman. You spoke to the Chairman?"

"And he invited me to a party." Absinthe suddenly brightens up. For days now, he's been carrying around the thought that Turtledove had another male interest, but now it's clear that this was just a mix-up. Plus, Turtledove is in good health, well rested, and he has a party to invite her too. He perks up and flashes one of his famous Rhinohorn smiles. "If you are feeling up to it, maybe you'd like to go to a party tomorrow night."

"A party?"

"You could be my plus-one." Absinthe hands over the envelope containing the invitation. Turtledove opens it, a suspicious look on her face. She reviews the details. It is indeed an invitation, but not to a party, it's an official cocktail event. There's nothing party-like about it. She tells absinthe, "You know that the Roman gladiators were often invited to parties with the elite?"

"Really?" That idea plays well with Absinthe, and his grin persists.

"But they were invited for entertainment, Absinthe. This is not a party, like the sort of drinking party you are used to. This is corporate networking event. The only reason you'd go to this is to either further the entity you are representing or to further your own career. This is not about fun. It is an environment, where you are being watched, observed and judged by whoever is in the room."

Absinthe is reminded of Turtledove's prickly, corporate, legalistic side and how she always manages to read complexities into things that are really quite simple.

"So, will you come?"

"Really, Absinthe. Me turning up with you would be fraught with risk, especially if we are thought to be an actual couple."

Absinthe sinks again. Then he remembers his pledge to support her, no matter what. So they'd go together, alone. That's fine. But Turtledove isn't finished with briefing him on the intricacies of his proposal.

"A corporate cocktail party is just a fancy board room; it is more nerve-wracking, as the playing field is far from even. It can be a trap for young players, loose lips sink ships; people are judging! Can one keep it together with the introduction of the acceptable social elixir of releasing the inner whoever you are; do people think you have the right mix of having fun but with enough social decorum; were you too uptight; the benchmark depends on the others' moral compass - these people are not your friends, Absinthe."

That comment strikes a nerve. He remembers when his Director said the same thing to him and yet walked him to the door on two occasions with his hand on his shoulder.

"There is no coming back from an alcohol induced act that is deemed as unfavourable in these circles, Absinthe. No, these events can be boardroom traps & people who are not used to them can be spotted a mile away."

"So will you come?" Absinthe repeats, convinced that keeping it simple and repetitive is the only option.

Turtledove mulls it over. "So you want me to go to what I have just described to you as a high stress environment the day after I get out of hospital?"

"*Ummm.*"

"You do, don't you?"

"*Ahhh.*"

"And is that an example of a man thinking of himself, or a man who is looking out for the interests of someone that he professes to care for?"

Before Absinthe can answer this life changing question there is a knock at the door, a nurse enters, and in the space of a minute, Absinthe is ushered out of the room, not to return until the following day.

He looks down at the white envelope in his hands and wonders what just happened, whether even he should attend the cocktail event, and whether it was even a good idea to invited Turtledove. The thoughts compound as he walks across the carpark and by the time he is sitting in the driver's seat, he is rendered practically catatonic by them.

He heaves a heavy sigh, taking stock of the few good things that have transpired. Turtledove is in good health, George is actually him, the Chong Triad will never threaten Turtledove again, and he has been invited to attend a fancy event at the top end of town. The big question is, has he been invited because he is entertaining, or for some other reason? Then the bigger question, is he going to go alone? If Turtledove declines, maybe he can take Horace. At least Horace will be able to interpret all the complexities that he now understands will be going on.

He is about to turn the key in the ignition when his text messenger beeps. He checks to see that he has an incoming from Turtledove. His heart flutters. The text message reads, "I'll come. But we have to have rules. I'll send through later.

No Tux, But I Have A Glock

The very concept of "I'll send the rules through later" is enough to send Absinthe into a tizz. He drives away from the hospital feeling, in the first instance, like he had won the lottery. In the next instant he thinks that maybe he won't like the rules of engagement. That said, Turtledove and Director Maidmont had already briefed him on the context: you are being set up, these are not your friends, advancement or destruction are equally possible. You take the risk in order to advance yourself or your organisation.

The concept is quite peculiar to Absinthe. How does he seek to advance himself? Just getting through a day alive is all the advancement he needs. And even more peculiar, the concept of advancing his organisation, how does that happen? The place is going to be crawling with Director-level people. What could he possibly do to advance the organisation?

Maybe all he has to do is show up, let everyone see what someone from the pointy end looks like, maybe regale them with some tales about ventilating crypto-rats. Civilians are often fascinated by combat, so Absinthe's job is simply to share some stories, pose for selfies with the directors like a poster boy for Bitcrime Division, the way a lead actor represents a whole movie and everyone in it.

He'll probably be all stiff and anxious if he goes in to that limelight stone-sober, so best that he knocks down a few rumbos before he gets there to in order to, you know, get into the swing of things. But don't get drunk. Hell no. Certainly don't get smashed. And no wrestling. Absolutely no wrestling. And maybe get a haircut, buzz-cut number two all around the shock of the slicked-back top hair. Maybe spend the day at the shooting range, let the Directors know what a real soldier smells like.

Absinthe takes the thought to another extreme. Maybe he could go to the cocktail event in combat fatigues. And take his gun! Hell, yeah! He could go in full battle dress, the body armour, the tricked-out MP5 assault rifle, Glock 19 semi-automatic pistol, trench knife, radio, and a tactical vest stuffed with hand grenades, smoke grenades, cyalume sticks, and a bunch of magazines loaded with fresh ammo.

As Absinthe is thinking these things, he hears his phone sound an incoming text message. It is from Turtledove, it says: "Do you have a tux?"

Absinthe chuckles, and quickly texts back, "No. But I got a Glock." But then he sees the point. He has absolutely no idea how to behave, or even to dress for this event. He wishes he hadn't sent that text and stands there feeling that familiar feeling that goes by the name of, "I've done it again."

"*Hmmm.*" Absinthe becomes contemplative and when his text message sounds again, his stomach cramps, thinking that he is going to be reprimanded in Turtledove's text. He looks at the message that reads, "Please don't bring any guns." Then another message arrives that simply says, "lol".

"Phew!" She saw the joke. Absinthe feels worn out. He feels as though his emotions are being yanked up and down like a yo-yo by a hyperactive kid who's been binge-drinking red cordial. Jumping out of helicopters with guns is so much more relaxing.

Absinthe decides that he best not over-think the cocktail event and let the experts get back to him with their recommendations in due course. And tuxedo, can he assume that he needs a tuxedo?

Rules of Engagement

At 6pm sharp, Absinthe Rhinohorn enters the lobby of Turtledove's hotel like a man transformed. He looks dashingly handsome in his dinner suit and bowtie, socks and polished shoes. His scalp practically shines, what with the number two comb having trimmed him right back. His flicked-back hair has an oily sheen and a slight coconut aroma from the product that the hairdresser used. Plus, he's wearing cologne, so there is absolutely no chance of him smelling of gunpowder, brick dust and blood. He had decided against taking two shots of rum, and settled on just one, although that's kind of the same thing, really.

Perhaps the most important thing of all that contributes to his handsomeness this evening is that he is happy. He's got that Rhinohorn smile. And when Rhinohorn smiles, the world smiles too.

He rubs his hands together and glances around the lobby, expecting to see Turtledove bounding towards him. He doesn't see her, but he does remember the list of conditions that she had asked him to agree to, in order that she would consent to being his plus-one. He pulls the sheet of folded paper out of his pocket, opens it, browses it, and replaces it. What a list! He was up half the night trying to get his head around it. Each bullet point needed its own deep contemplation, impact assessment and operational plan. The list was stifling, to say the least. But with that said, despite having being practically gelded, emasculated, straight-jacketed, hand-cuffed and incarcerated by the rules of engagement, he is, after-all, going on a date with Turtledove!

Except that it's not a date! No. No. Of course. What was he thinking? That's been made abundantly clear. They don't interact like that, anymore. Hell no. And rightly so.

"And rightly so," says Absinthe, aloud with an unconvincing tone.

Their relationship has matured considerably since the time when they were periodically engaging in steamy sexual trysts in wind-swept beach shacks, caravans, and under a truck in a mangrove forest.

Oh, yes, the relationship between Turtledove and Absinthe Rhinohorn has gone from strength to strength since those sordid, debauched, awesome and amazing days. It has positively mushroomed - he had been recently informed - now that they are not bed-fellows, and now the relationship between them could be best described as friends, work mates, professional associates, and former-lovers.

No! No! Strike that last one. That's not part of the official script. There will be no reference to them having been intimate. None. What was he thinking?

Absinthe sighs, feeling the mind-miles coming on. He's finding it hard to decipher between his extinction-imminent way of interpreting events, and the thoughts that have been sown into his head, supposedly for benefit of relationship sustainability.

 Absinthe glances at his wristwatch, confirms that he is on time and Turtledove is running five minutes late.

Then he sees Turtledove. She's engaged in an intense conversation with Director Maidmont. Absinthe approaches, then becomes unsure of himself. What were the rules of engagement, again? He retrieves the document from his pocket, swots up, replaces it, and ponders what to do next. Most relevant is Article 6 that firmly states: "I wish to be treated with the utmost respect and there is to be no pressure applied to be anything more than good professional friends." So how would good professional friends behave in this situation? Well, Absinthe thinks, he might just saunter over there and join in, right?

Wrong, as he approaches, Turtledove and Director Maidmont hurriedly complete their conversation, with The Director saying, "I'll see if I can get to the Chairman right away." The two women observe Absinthe's approach. The Director says, "Hello, Mr Rhinohorn. You do look very dashing tonight."

Absinthe is about to reply, "Thank you darling, you look quite a dish, yourself," but he catches himself, and instead extends his hand formally to shake, "Good evening, Director." Then he turns his attention to Turtledove and feels like he is not inappropriate to stoop forward and place a kiss - a very respectful and professional kiss - on her cheek. He thinks that this is appropriate as it will allow her to gauge that he is not emanating any malodours.

"Hello Absinthe," Turtledove is pleasantly surprised at how well George of the Jungle scrubs up.

"I'll see you at the event." Director Maidmont makes her departure.

Absinthe and Turtledove stand there looking at each other for a few moments before she says, "Did you get a car?"

"I got a stretch limo."

"You didn't need to get a stretch."

"Oh, really?"

Outside the lobby there waits the black stretch limousine. The chauffer greets them, pulls open the door and ushers them inside.

Seated inside the plush leather seats, Absinthe asks, "How are you? Turtledove? What happened over there?"

Turtledove explains, "No sooner had I stepped into my office than there was this terrible crash and I blacked out. When I came too, I was on a stretcher being carted out of this ruined buildings. The doctors thought that I might have a concussion, so they ordered me to days of bed rest and observation. But I am okay now. I'm all good."

"Well the guys that fired the rocket won't be doing that again."

"So I heard, and thank you for intervening like that, it was beyond the call. And look, something quite extraordinary has come out of it. We get to meet the Chairman."

"That's a good thing, isn't it?"

"If we play it right, it's a very good thing."

"I think that he likes me," says Absinthe, thoughtfully.

"You might have solved a problem for him. That doesn't make you his friend, Absinthe."

"I'm not so good with all this corporate relationship stuff," Absinthe mumbles.

"Well, tonight you are in safe hands," Turtledove reassures him, placing her hand and on his wrist and giving it a little squeeze, "Because I am excellent at it."

The Cocktail Event

Despite his misgivings and anxieties about the event, Absinthe immediately feels himself to be comfortable and at home. Certainly he looks different to the general crowd, he is bigger - both taller and wider- he has a shaved head. And he has a general look of someone who ought to be shown utmost respect as he is quite capable of razing the entire building and turning every item in the room into a deadly weapon.

Rather than standing in the side of the room not knowing who to talk to or why, Absinthe finds a constant stream of well-meaning people want to speak to him. Turtledove is always close by, dressed in a blue Carla Zampatti cocktail dress and very high heels; presenting just the right amount of corporate sexiness. At one stage, there is a group of about eight people surrounding them both. Some social innovator has cottoned onto Absinthe's name and has rustled a tray of Absinthe cocktails. The drink become a topic of hot debate.

Then the Director of Bitcrime Division shows up. He makes a big fuss over Absinthe, drapes an arm around his shoulder and regales the audience with the tale about what Absinthe did to the crypto-rat in the porta-loo. *Ahhh*, that mission seems like it was an age ago. Absinthe thinks that he ought to correct the Director's story by saying that it was Helmet who ventilated the crypto-rat, against a direct order, and that he had nearly been shot dead, himself, because of it. But Absinthe is learning that there is the 'true story' there is the 'good story' and there is the 'official story'. And tonight is the night of the good story.

Then, there is an announcement, and all eyes turn towards the where the Chairman is being introduced.

"There's your mate," grins Turtledove, gently nudging her elbow into his ribs.

Absinthe glances down at her that ridiculous Rhinohorn grin plastered all over his face. He sees her petite frame, her hair draped over her shoulders and that angelic face, and he feels himself to be falling in towards her like he was a celestial body being drawn towards a radiant planet by the inexorable force of gravity. "He scrubs up alright, don't he, that Rhinohorn," he thinks. Maybe the meteor didn't extinct the Turtledove relationship after-all, and it just got a bit just singed it. And who said that he was unable to think of someone else, or to do things that benefitted his life. Let's face it, Turtledove wasn't on the invite list to this prestigious event until Absinthe invited her as his plus-one. And here she is as his partner. Is that the right word? Maybe tonight is the big comeback!

This extinction-level thought – naïve, deluded, irrational and frankly, near-suicidal, as it is – buoys Absinthe, and he materialises the thought by shuffling a pace closer towards Turtledove. However, he doesn't sense that she instinctively shuffles a pace away from him, in order to keep the space between them at that 'respectful, professional friends' distance. He doesn't pick this up because he is distracted by the sight of the Chairman stepping up onto the stage. And because he doesn't pick this up, the thought continues to flicker through the ethanol-soaked, lizard-like part of his brain that he uses to contemplate matters of the heart. He so foolishly persists in the belief that Turtledove has actually accepted his advance. What could possibly go wrong?

The Chairman's Speech

The Chairman moves to a raised podium, behind which is the Department of Planetary Boundaries Defence seal. This is a brightly coloured image of planet Earth rotating with the department's name written around the outside. This is all set within a blue circle, and at the bottom of the seal, there is a circle with a sniper's crosshairs, letting it be known with no uncertainty that this is a department with murderous intent.

The departmental seal looks like a halo around the Chairman's head, giving the impression that not only is he powerful, but that he is enlightened. It's all very deliberate stage-craft on his part, and it serves an important corporate purpose, as well as tickling his over-inflated, old-man's ego.

He begins his presentation, "Well, the weather certainly tuned it on for us tonight, around the world. A fifth, category-6 hurricane in as many weeks lashes mainland United States. Ice-storms in Europe. Bushfires and drought in what used to be the Amazon rainforest. And floods, exacerbated by rising seas in Bangladesh. Pity poor Bangladesh. How many people perished from extreme weather, today? Ten thousand? A hundred thousand? Do we do climate change body counts anymore?""

He lets the question hang in the air for a little while, allowing the audience settle and prepare for what comes next.

"You know, it was with no great joy that my team and I outlined the necessity and the function of the Department of Planetary Boundaries Defence to the few enlightened national governments who took the time to listen to us. It gave me no pleasure at all, to recommend a shoot-on-sight policy for perpetrators of environmental crime. Certainly, we have body-count as one of our operational KPI's, but it is with a heavy heart that I review progress through those grim statistics. But it had to happen. Governments have been glacially slow to act on long-term threats. In fact, ironically, the glaciers proved to move much faster." He chuckles at his own joke, and this encourages a laugh to spread around the auditorium.

"My, how fast those glaciers move! Then at the last, it became abundantly clear to the enlightened governments that the prognoses of climate scientists and those who study the whole systems of Earth, dating back to the eighties, and who had been roundly ignored all along, were actually correct. All that bad news was coming true and much faster than we had anticipated. And now what do we do? Well, as it happens, it became necessary to eradicate some humans in order to save humanity. It wasn't about reducing population numbers, over-all, as some suggest. After-all, who wanted to tell the rich-west that if we are going to shoot people in order to reduce net ecological-footprint, that 'they' would be first against the wall because of their huge per capita consumption. No, much better to focus the pointy end on the perpetrators of environmental crime."

The Chairman clears his throat and then resumes his speech.

"So around the world, day-by-day, this department oversees the eradication of human beings caught red-handed perpetrating eco-crimes such as cryptocurrency mining, in order that we mitigate climate change; wildlife trafficking, to protect biosphere integrity; using more that the regulation amount of nitrogen fertilizer, to protect the oceans from dead-zones; and releasing refrigerant gasses into the atmosphere, to help repair the ozone layer. And so on and so forth. Nine planetary boundaries, and over fifty designated eco-crimes, and more on the way. Bang! Bang! Bang! Bang! Bang!" He pounds his fist against the lectern at this point, sending a jolt of anxiety through the audience.

"I tell you, it gives me no joy to see the photos of those poor, young men ventilated for environmental crime. But if it helps to prevent the extinction of the human race and most organisms bigger than an earthworm, I'd blow the little bastard's brains out myself!"

The Chairman sighs, seeming like he has made himself anxious. He shuffles his notes and casts his eyes around furtively as if looking for the place to regain his speech. The top of his head is shiny bald, and all round the back and sides, the hair is fine and white. When he is flustered, like this, the white hair seems to stand on end, like an alarmed cat, so from a distance, his head seems to glow.

"Yes. It certainly is unfair that the little people should be the ones to suffer the pointy end. And for that reason, the department is investing new effort in ensuring that the big people get a taste of our unique wall of fire. This brings with it added complications because big people are always protected by powerful people. But there is a new zeitgeist in the world today. And it says that the powerful people are fair game for their complicity in environmental crime. So the rich man or poor, powerful or weak, if you perpetrate planet-crime, watch out, we have ninjas everywhere."

The Chairman lightens his tone considerably, almost glad to have gotten through the grim part of his tale.

"Yes, we have all manner of good people working with our department. We have planners, and bureaucrats, people to develop policy and those who execute policy. Indeed, we have a very proficient executioner in the audience today." The Chairman glances down at Absinthe, as he says this, and Absinthe doesn't know which way to look. "I can see that many of you have met him, and that you are practically drinking him up." The Chairman brings his glass into view. It, like many others in the room, contains the green Absinthe cocktail. "Cheers to you, brave, committed man." The Chairman raises his glass in salute and takes a swig.

Absinthe is rendered speechless, he looks around anxiously, not knowing how to behave. He glances at Turtledove who winks at him as if to say, "It's okay, relax. You did well."

"Anyway," the Chairman concludes. "I'm not here to bore you with my stories. You know the drill. You get free booze in exchange for listening to some old fart bag on. Well, I'm all done here. Eat, drink, and be merry. Tomorrow, we go back to the trenches."

The Chairman steps off the podium, and instantly the sound of chatter fills the air.

Absinthe watches him, fascinated until he disappears from view in the crowd.

"*Huh!*" says Turtledove, taken aback by it all. "You certainly did make an impression on the Chairman."

"That's a good thing, right?"

"On balance, I'd say, yes."

Planning and Execution

Following the Chairman's speech and the announcement that there is a friendly executioner in their midst, Absinthe is positively regaled by interested parties. "How big is your pistol?" one of the suited people ask, "Have you killed?" another asks, gravely. Initially, Absinthe is made anxious by all this newfound interest and to settle his nerves, he takes hold of a green cocktail from a passing waiter, skulls it, and grabs a second for justin - just in case, that is. He glances around to keep track of Turtledove and sees that she is a few paces away, engaged in an intense conversation with Director Maidmont. When he turns back to his eager audience, he sees his Bitcrime Division Director moving towards him with an entourage of his own. He interjects himself into Absinthe's personal space, then practically commands his presence like he owned the local franchise. The Director, clearly one green cocktail past his use-by date announces, "So if you absolutely need any motherfucker knocked off, bumped off, eradicated, terminated, murdered or shot, Absinthe Rhinohorn is your weapon of choice. We use him for all our big jobs."

Then he does that annoying thing where he drapes his arm over Absinthe's shoulder as if he really actually gave a fuck. Initially, Absinthe is accepting of this praise, but then he sees the Chairman doing his rounds, expertly, moving in his direction. Then the Chairman is right there and Absinthe freezes as their eyes meet. The Chairman, too, has an entourage. These people are seniors in the organisation, calm, resplendent in their corporate yet social attire. There are also seniors from other governmental departments and the private sphere. Close-up, the Chairman seems quite small and the crown of white hair very fine.

"If we're not interrupting," says the Chairman. "I'd like my associates to meet the pointy end of Bitcrime Division. To the extent that we are the gun, here is the bullet. I'm so glad you could come along, Absinthe Rhinohorn." The Chairman extends his hand and Absinthe shakes.

"Maybe I jump in here for a selfie," the Chairman sidles alongside Absinthe and of his staff raises a camera. "You have exactly the opposite hair to me," he comments then raises a fist and grins. Absinthe does likewise. Click! The camera captures the moment. "That one is going into the internal newsletter."

"What will we title it?" asks the photographer.

"Planning and execution."

Then the Director of Bitcrime Division makes a comment about the day that he signed Absinthe to the team, and Absinthe makes the classic mistake of rewarding him by turning his face towards. And in that moment, the Chairman ambles off into the crowd.

Then the Bitcrime Director starts mouthing off about a subject that all the remaining folk can relate to: the night that the whole city was blacked out.

"I remember that," says one. "I was washing my hair in the bath and the whole house went black."

"It was out for hours," says another.

"Well, I can explain that," the Director says. He turns to Absinthe, "Do you mind?"

"Operational collateral damage," Absinthe shrugs. "It's no biggie."

"So, Absinthe here is set loose with his team of mercenaries to eradicate a nest of crypto-rats who had set up in an old warehouse out back of the industrial district."

"What does that mean?" one asks.

"Crypto-miners," says the Director. "Wasting electricity for no good reason."

"Well good riddance to them," says another.

"Anyway," continues the Director, "In the heat of battle. Absinthe accidentally opens up with his MP5 machine gun and spouts fifteen rounds of 9mm ammo into this $12.6 million pad-mount transformer that promptly goes *kaboom*!" The Director emphasises with the wave of his arms. "And shortly thereafter, I get saddled with biggest damned power-bill in human history." The Director is rewarded with considerable laughter from his audience, and when it dies down, he completes, "But you took care of that, didn't you, Absinthe."

"Indeed I did," Absinthe agrees. Then he takes hands his cocktail to the Director, to free him up to perform some showmanship. "I am fire power!" Absinthe growls, striking a martial-arts karate pose, and causing every one of his swooning groupies to step back in shock. He executes a rapid right-left-right punch in the air, his dinner jacket making a distinctive slapping noise, and him grunting with each slamming air punch. He resumes the relaxed position, clasps his hands together and bows to his audience.

The audience breaks into applause, having just witnessed the most exciting event of the whole evening. Absinthe is suddenly surrounded by friends, and he retrieves his self-named cocktail, tips it down his neck and is immediately rewarded with another. The noise of the chatter rises and Absinthe loses interest. He glances around for Turtledove. She is a little way away and engaged in a heated and animated debate with Director Maidmont and the Chairman.

"That's odd," he thinks, paying particular attention to the body language. It seems like Turtledove and Director Maidmont are trying to convince the Chairman of something that he is reluctant to believe. Then the Chairman waves his hand in frustration and departs, his entourage swallowing him up.

"How strange," thinks Absinthe. Then it gets stranger still. The Chairman returns with two senior and serious looking folk who interrogate Director Maidmont while Turtledove nods her head approvingly. There is a heated five-way debate and finally the Chairman reaches a decision, shakes Director Maidmont's hand and then turns his attention to Turtledove. He takes both her hands in his and leans forward to speak to her almost intimately. Turtledove responds in kind and then they are both nodding as if having come to final negotiated agreement. Then the Chairman recedes back into the crowd. Absinthe watches as Turtledove and Director Maidmont hug and almost seem to share a tear. Then the Director departs, and Turtledove looks around for what comes next. She sees Absinthe looking at her and she walks towards him, through the fawning entourage and rests by his side.

"Are you okay?" he asks.

"Yeah. You?"

"Yes. It is fun."

"There is no pressure on you to leave anytime soon, but I have done what I need to do here now, so happy to leave at any time."

"Where do you want to go to?"

"Home," she says, and poor-old deluded Absinthe thinks that she means back to his squalid, damp, sock-smelling apartment, when in fact she meant back to a room in the Hilton, on her own. What a misunderstanding! What could possibly go wrong?

"We should go now."

"Now? Are you sure? Aren't you enjoying your-self? I can wait on."

"Oh, no," he says. "I think that I have advanced my-self enough here, tonight."

With that, they turn, and Absinthe places his hand in the small of her back as they walk towards the door.

Cherry Tree Avenue

Inside the limousine, Absinthe presses the intercom button and advises the chauffer that they are going to Cherry Tree Avenue, back to his squalid apartment. He resumes his seat and sees Turtledove observing at him with an amused look.

"I guess I should have added a wee extra bullet point to the list."

"What would that have been?"

"You drop me off, not I drop you off," she chuckles as she says this.

"Drop you off?"

"Yes, drop me off at my hotel after the event."

"Drop you off? I thought that you wanted to come back?" Absinthe says, confused.

"Come back? Come back where?"

"Come back to my apartment for, you know..."

"Where-ever did you get that idea from?"

"Isn't that what this is about?"

"What on Earth are you thinking?" Turtledove is visibly surprised.

"I thought that we were back together."

"Back together? What are you even talking about?"

"Well, I did everything on the list."

"It's nothing to do with the damned list, Absinthe! That was to keep your ass safe in a hostile environment."

"But I took you to the cocktail event. I got you a ticket."

"I already had a ticket from my Director. I came along so that you didn't end up getting fired."

"So we're not getting back together?"

"Together? We never were together, you big lunk."

"Then what were we?"

"We weren't anything. Oh, Absinthe, why don't you listen," Turtledove is visibly annoyed. "We were just intimate for a period and then we moved on. That's all."

"We moved on?" stammers Absinthe, distraught. "You mean you moved on. I'm still stuck here."

Turtledove fixes him with a glare. "Yes. Absinthe. I moved on and you are still stuck here. Like a wee elephant in the mud. Extricate yourself."

Absinthe lowers his head, crest-fallen. He's got that voice in his head again. "I've done it again." But he's not sure what he's done. He's misread something simple, and now it's got all complicated. But this time, it's all too much. He feels like he has been punched in the gut – by someone strong, like Horace. The Absinthe cocktails – all four of them – are probably not helping him think clearly.

It's all too much for him. He wants to get off. He leans forward, and presses the switch to slide open the hatch to the chauffer.

"Pull over here, mate," he instructs the driver, gruffly. The vehicle pulls to a halt and Absinthe moves towards the door. "I can't stay," he tells Turtledove, honestly.

"I understand."

He pushes the door open, and the cabin is infused with the smell of the rain. A waft of cold air brings in the sparkling sensation of wispy water droplets.

"You know that you don't have to hurt yourself every time you fail to get what you want," Turtledove says, as an olive branch, hoping that he won't follow through on his plan.

Absinthe nods, more in acknowledgement that he has heard what she said, than that he agrees with her. He steps out into the rain, and just stands there looking at the ground. The water lands on his head makes a cold rivulet that penetrates his dry clothes and runs down his spine.

"Jump back in the car, Absinthe," she tries, one last time. Seconds pass and he hears he door close behind him, and the vehicle pull away. The rivulet becomes a stream, then an icy torrent. He lets out a deep sigh and turns to see the limousine make a U-turn, a little way into the distance. As the vehicle approaches, Absinthe looks mournfully at the black tinted windows and the second that the vehicle has passed it occurs to him that he has just performed one of the most stupid acts of his life.

In that moment that he sees the taillights, he is stuck with the need for instant action. He's not letting Turtledove go like that. He is going to see her safely to her hotel lobby, receive a small kiss on the cheek, turn and never see her again. That's how this things plays out. She's just got out of the hospital, for crying out loud! What were you thinking, Absinthe?

In order to make that happen, he needs to arrest the motion of that limousine. In order to do that, he needs to break his inertia and run.

Run, Absinthe, run, like you integrity and goodness depends on it.

In a violent burst of action, Absinthe begins an intense sprint. The vehicle is fifty meters away and accelerating. If Absinthe is to catch up, he must travel faster that it is travelling, and quickly, too. He pumps every ounce of available energy into his rapid acceleration, moving immediately into anaerobic respiration. Pam! Pam! Pam! His feet slam into the wet road, rain lashing his face. He closes the distance between him and the limo but knows that it will outpace him. He can't run to the front of it, but he can alert the driver by slamming a fist against the boot. Pam! Pam! Pam! He crashes forward, and at that last moment, leaps forward, his right hand raised, ready to give the boot one hell of a walloping. He descends, his face lashed by the rain, brings his arm down, and missed the back of the vehicle by just an inch and lands heavily, face first in the road.

He leaps to his feet, shakes water off his face, raises his arms in the air and screams an agonised howl, *"Raaaarrgh!!"*

But it is not enough to alert the driver, and the limousine speeds on, its tail-lights making little ruby coloured sparkles glitter in the rain. Absinthe stands there, feeling as if all the component parts of his body are being turned to liquid and are being washed down the gutters by the rain.

Why? Why? Why?

Absinthe walks in the rain, his thoughts cycling and tripping over one another. Why did he assume that Turtledove wanted him back? WTF? Why couldn't he see the signs? Why did he have to throw a hissy fit in the limo, when he could have just been cool honey-bunny? Why? Why? Why?

He feels as though he has had a brief, fleeting moment at the front of the queue, then sent all the way to the back again by his own inadequacies. For just seconds he had viewed the verdant plateau at the top of the hill, the broad vista of sunlit meadows, flowers, and an enchanting forest, beyond. Then he lost his footing and slid through the mud, all the way to the bottom. What a waste. What a flop. What a complete farce of a man.

Absinthe falls into a dark place as he walks, staring at the wet pavement. He doesn't consciously know where he is going; he's on autopilot. Maybe he's on his way back the elevator in the basement level carpark. Or maybe he is marching back to the weak spot in the nuclear reactor via an armoury where he will retrieved a big gun loaded with armour piercing bullets. And what would be the outcome of that? He'd detonate a nuclear reactor. It would be like a dirty bomb going off on the outskirts of his city. Why would he inflict that on other people? Why would he do that? Why would he even think that? That seems to be the problem - the things that he thinks. Maybe he should stop doing that.

Through the dark storm clouds inside his mind, the terrain is momentarily illuminated by a strike of lightning. "It's not your fault," that's what Dr Stent told him, and he should know as he's a damned heart specialist.

"It's not my fault," Absinthe says aloud, trying on the affirmation to see if it fits.

"It's not my fault!" he bellows, standing there in the dark, calling into the rain.

This buoys him considerably, and he picks up his pace. "Don't stop trying. Prepare for misfires," the Doctor had said. But no mention of complete cluster-fucks like tonight.

Absinthe stops. He pulls the bullet list out of his pocket and squints at it under a streetlight for as long as it remains intact, then it gets soggy and falls apart in his hands. Nowhere in there does it specify that Turtledove's attending the event meant that she would accompany him to his apartment afterwards. Nowhere. It's a fabrication. He made it up. "What the hell was he even thinking?" Thinking. There's that word again.

Absinthe finds himself in a familiar place. He is standing outside the Bazooka Bar. The last thing he remembers of that night is ordering a nitro-glycerine cocktail.

Toothbrush and a Bullet Casing

Absinthe wakes with a heavy and fast beating heart. He lays there, wondering what woke him. His head hurts from too much booze, and he rises, desperate to drink water. As he stumbles through the apartment, he comes across something most odd. On the kitchen table is a note that reads," Awesome night, RH. CU soon. M." And then a telephone number.

The note is perplexing in itself, but what is most odd is the way the note is presented. It is written on a blank sheet and pinned to the table with a collection of items that have been harvested from various places around the apartment. There is a little monument comprising a silver teaspoon resting on a toothbrush, an empty bullet casing, and the plastic flower, all arranged deliberately.

Absinthe is perplexed. There are two explanations for this. First, he has met someone last night who wrote the note, then he travelled home with it - in the rain - perfectly preserved and built a monument to it on the table. Certainly, he's done some pretty fucked-up things, drunk, but never art! Alternatively, someone was here with him last night who wrote the note and made the statue and then departed. Which was it? Absinthe can't remember. In fact, the last thing that he remembers is raised a fifty-dollar bill and ordering a nitro-glycerine cocktail spiced with a shot of Absinthe. As if Absinthe really needed any more Absinthe!

Perplexed by these discoveries, Absinthe shuffles into the bathroom where he sees his drenched dinner suit in a pool on the floor and a note-to-self written on the mirror in Turtledove's fuchsia lipstick. The note incompletely reads, "It's not your…" But he knows what it means.

He's feeling philosophical about his blow up with Turtledove and determined not to let it drag him down. He wonders whether he should check on her, to make sure she got home safe, but then he thinks that he needs to let go. "You have to stop pursuing her," he tells himself. And then he is conflicted, because if he cared for her the way he professed, then he would confirm that she got home safe. Or would he only be doing that to appear to be caring? This train of thoughts is exhausting, and Absinthe returns to the main room only to be confused by the art work on the kitchen table.

The day is shaping up to be a horror show, and Absinthe searches around for something to distract him. His phone is lying on the floor. He observes that he has calls and messages. There is a text from Turtledove, "I'm home safe. Thanks for asking. You?"

Absinthe eases a sigh of relief. That shipping container full of anxiety can now be put to one side. And the phone calls: eight from Horace. That's eight. From Horace!

Absinthe calls him right back and car barely hear what he is saying because the earpiece is drenched with rainwater. Horace's garbled voice sounds like an octopus gurgling liquefied jellyfish, but Absinthe is able to gain the following information: Horace has tracked down the Love Coin miners and time is short ventilate them. Great news! Something to distract him from the miasma of anxieties that never seem to go away.

The New Guy

Absinthe arrives at Bitcrime Division HQ to get briefed by Horace and prepare for combat. The first thing he observes is that one of his team is missing.

"Where's Carly?"

"Carly has gone to Mars," Horace tells him. "She got the call and bailed for induction at short notice. So we got this new guy."

The new guy looks a bit too nerdy for the pointy end of Bitcrime. "He isn't going to last long," mutters Absinthe.

The new guy looks up from the operational log-book. "So, we're shooting crypto-miner's, right?"

"That's right."

"Sounds a bit extreme, but I guess if it keeps the price of video cards down, it's probably not a bad thing. But I don't understand why you didn't shoot these guys mining NXT tokens."

"You shoot who we tell you to shoot," grumbles Helmet, strapping on his body armour.

"I'll tell you why, mate," Horace offers. "You see, not all cryptos are mined. There are other ways to create them. Cryptos that are mined use shitloads of energy and that's carbon."

"So what's so different about mining?"

"Well in the mining, there's this thing called 'Difficulty' you see. The more people mining it, the more difficult they make it to mine, which is to say more electricity, which is to say more carbon emissions, and the planet dies faster. You following me?"

"I think so."

"So, if value of the coin goes up, more people pile in to mine it, to make a buck, the difficulty goes up, the energy consumption of the mining network goes up – the whole thing goes exponential. So, if a crypto gets to be worth million bucks each, the mining network will be sucking 15% of global electricity supply and that's a shit-load of carbon."

"Alright, mofos," Absinthe claps his hands together. "Let's get this briefing underway."

Horace addresses the team. "We've got this new crypto out there called Love Coin. These greedy little bastards are mining crypto on pacemakers. Now, unlike the mining I've just been telling you about that gets its power from the mains network – mainly coal powered – this one has a miniscule power demand, provided by the pulsing flow of blood. So it's not a carbon threat, it's a health threat. And while that it technically outside the scope of Bitcrime Division--"

"That's a lot of that going on, recently," mumbles Helmet.

Horace continues, "We're going to track these crypto-rats down anyway."

The new guy puts his hand in the air.

"Yes, mate."

"Are we going to ventilate them, too?"

"Yes, mate. We are going to ventilate them. Now, we've got a three-hour chopper ride. Slide down a rope. Jump through a window and shoot anything that moves. Simples. Any questions. Absinthe."

"Are they armed?"

"We have to assume so. Helmet?"

"Are they mining other coin?"

"Yes, mate. They are running a medium-density multi-coin farm, we estimate drawing around two megawatts. There's probably ten to fifteen rats in there need ventilating."

Can I Ask You Something?

Later, at the hide-out where the Love Coin miners are located, the pointy end of Bitcoin Division crouch behind a wall and check weapons. The rain falls and Absinthe glances around to see his team lined up behind him.

"Alright, I'll go in first," he says. "You guys stay on my tail." He glances around the wall, but rather than having a clear-eye operational reconnoitre, he thinks of Turtledove. "Stand by," he tells his team. "Stand by. Stand by. Go! Go! Go!"

Absinthe rushes towards the door, plants his foot in the middle, but the damned door refuses to open. So he boots it three times before it finally falls in. This delay is all the time that is needed to alert the crypto-rats inside, and as soon as Absinthe is in the empty door-frame, there is a volley of gunfire and he is immediately struck by three rounds that punch hard into his bulletproof vest – right in the centre, right over his heart. The bullets throw him heavily onto the ground, and he lays there, winded, gasping for air.

Helmet and the new guy leap over him, into the building. The open up with three-round bursts from their MP5s. There is the sound of screaming as bullets impact into machines and flesh.

Horace rushes over to the dazed Absinthe, "What the fuck are you doing, you clumsy bastard?"

"I'm got a bit distracted mate."

"You can't get distracted at the pointy end!"

"Can I ask you something?" Absinthe grips Horace by the arm, desperate to speak.

The sound of gunfire continues to rattle off inside the building. It's the disciplined sound of the MP5s, and the occasional erratic burst from a low-powered pistol. It's the noise you hear when Bitcrime Division is routing the crypto-rats. Horace wants to join in, but Absinthe holds him back, gripping his arm tightly.

"*Ahhh*, fuck it," Horace says. "Helmet can show the new boy around. What is it? Is this about your side-mission?"

"Yeah," Absinthe is desperate to tell his story.

"Let me guess. It's another shambolic, ham-fisted love affair gone sour?"

Absinthe blushes - and that doesn't happen very often. "Have a look at this." He retrieves his mobile and opens the email showing Turtledove's bullet-list. He asks, "If I got full marks, does this mean that she'd take me back?"

"What is this?" asks Horace.

"It's the rules of engagement for her to be my plus-one at a cocktail event with the Chairman."

"You got invited to a cocktail event with the Chairman? And you didn't invite me?"

"Just look at the damned list, will you?"

Horace shakes his head wearily, then reads from the screen, "Number 1. *Pick me up from the hotel in a driven street car*. What's that mean? What's a driven street car?"

"It's a limousine."

"Did you do that?"

"Yeah. I got a stretch. But she said she didn't need a stretch."

"So you fucked that up? The first one? The very first one? Not off to a good start, hey Absinthe?"

"Half marks, maybe?"

"Okay, number 2. *In the car, debrief of Absinthe's goals for the evening along with an idea of who will be there*. Did you do that?"

There is the sound of a grenade going off inside the building and Horace looks up.

"It's okay, it's one of ours," Absinthe tells him.

"So did you do that?"

"Sort of."

"Sort of?

"I don't have goals. If I wake up in the morning, I've done well. I got invited, I wanted to be with her, that's it."

"Did you tell her that?"

"Not in so many words."

"Well, you get zero for number 2, then. Number 3. This is so funny. *Cleanliness: hair, teeth and antiperspirant. Breath mints.*"

"I did that. I still got the breath mints, see." Absinthe retrieves the box from his pants pocket.

Horace shakes his head, disappointed. "It's unopened, you fucking dotard. You're supposed to put them in your mouth, not keep them in your pocket."

"Oh. I did brush my teeth, though."

"Good boy!"

"And I got a haircut."

"Half marks for that, then. Number 4. *Appropriate lounge suit and tie, socks and shoes (polished).*"

"Full marks. I get full marks for that one," Absinthe perks up a little.

"Number 5. This one isn't looking good."

"Is that the drinking one?"

"Yeah. *I expect you to be sober when I meet up with you.*" Horace starts laughing. "Boy, you are so out of your depth." He keeps reading, "*And one drink per hour thereafter - this is an executive social 'meeting' and responsible social drinking is to be observed.* Not a fucking chance! So how much did you drink?"

Just then, one of the cryptocurrency miners appears in the door way. He sees Horace and Absinthe, panics, and runs for his life. Absinthe retrieves his Glock 19, fires three rounds into his back, kills the crypto-rat, and then fesses up to Horace. "I had four drinks in two hours."

"What sort of drinks?"

"Cocktails."

"So you had at least eight standard drinks in two hours."

"Yeah, I guess I failed that one."

"Failed? You get negative one for that one, you piss-head. Number 6. *I wish to be treated with the utmost respect and there is to be no pressure applied to be anything more than good professional friends.*" Horace shakes his head, wearily. "You are so far out of your league with this woman. Who is she, she sounds like a lawyer. I'm assuming that you fucked that up, too."

"In the car on the way home. I thought she wanted to come back to my room."

"And she didn't, obviously. So what did you do?"

"I got out of the car."

"Well there's another negative one you dopey mutt. Number 7. *The car will wait and can be used by me at any time - as I am still convalescing.* You get a point there. Number 8. *I might think of more before the debriefing in the car.* No points to be awarded. Finally, number 9. *Don't make a fool out yourself and do not make one of me!* How do you think you went there?"

"Fucked it completely," moans Absinthe.

"Well, at least you're honest. I'll be kind and give you a zero for that one. So, to tally-up, out of a possible eight, you scored negative one and a half. Does that help explain your situation?"

"Thanks, Horace."

"You want some advice?"

Absinthe doesn't answer as he slides his phone and the unopened mints into his pocket and struggles to get up from the dirt.

"Here's my advice whether you want it or not, you old bastard. Keep trying. You can't fuck it up forever."

The sound of gun fire inside the building ceases and shortly, the entire building resonates with a powerful BOOM!! as the crypto-mining rigs are blown up. Then Helmet and the new guy appear in the doorway.

"What the fuck are you doing out here?" asks Helmet.

"Waiting on you," Absinthe says. "You all done?"

"All done, boss."

"How was that, mate?" Horace asks the new guy.

"Yeah, that was alright, hey. Is it like this every day?"

"On a good day," Absinthe tells him.

An Overgrown Mushroom

It is dusk as the Bitcrime Division team chopper back from the mission. Absinthe sits, staring at the floor, melancholically, thinking through his negative one and a half out of a possible eight score. It's nice at last to have some numbers to put to what has otherwise been a qualitative mess. Negative one and a half is better than negative two, he thinks, and this buoys him, a little.

As the chopper purrs towards home, he thinks that he really doesn't want to go back to his apartment. Instead, he needs some Absinthe-time alone, somewhere he can get his thoughts together. He has the helicopter set down in the big paddock in the grounds of the Department of Planetary Boundaries Defence.

"I'm just going to chill out here, for a while," he tells Horace as he steps out of the chopper, into the rain, taking with him just a poncho. He watches the helicopter alight and when it is out of sight, he finds a patch of grass that suits his mood. The rain is falling, and he dons the poncho, then sits.

He crosses his legs together to get settled, inhales, exhales deeply and then lowers his head to look at the grass being pattered by the rain.

Absinthe sits this way as the sun goes down beneath the grey clouds, slowly, gradually bringing on the gloom of night. And he sits that way through the darkness of the night. The noise of the rain pattering on the poncho keeps him awake, but eventually he nods off. He wakes periodically to the sound of foxes and quails or whatever noise-making wildlife have managed to avoid extinction in this part of the world. He is fast asleep, and motionless like a mushroom, when dawn arrives, and a figure appears out of the hazy, dim air.

He looks up with a start, observing the figure approach. She is carrying a large umbrella, the sort that doesn't invert or break in the wind. She wears her corporate raincoat and stands there protected from the swirling rain but being tickled by spindrift. It's Turtledove, standing there in the middle of the field.

"I wanted to see you before I left. And to had to walk into the middle of a paddock in a storm to do it."

Absinthe continues to look at the patch of grass in front of him. That's consistent with the sort of abuse he has dished out to the poor girl since he'd know her.

"I heard about what you did," Turtledove tells him, directly.

"What did I do?" Absinthe assumes that she's found evidence of more misdemeanours. He's completely lost track of them all, so can't fathom what it might be.

"You defended my honour, Absinthe. You took extreme risk to both your body and your career. And you annihilated the people who harmed me so that they would not do it again. And through your actions, you have made possible a mission that I designed but have been thwarted in executing."

"I don't understand."

"For years. We have been hitting the little people and, as a rule, letting the powerful ones go free. I have long argued that we need to take the fight to the top. Well, the Chairman has conceded that, significantly buoyed by the success of your Hong Kong job. He has given my mission the go ahead. I want to say thank you. I am in the place where I want to be now. And I wouldn't be there if it wasn't for you."

He looks up at Turtledove.

"Smile Absinthe. This is the good bit. From now on, the focus of my work will be to knock off the big guys, the corporate COE's who knowingly harm the environment. The Government ministers who yield such woeful policies. The little people will be arrested. But the rich and powerful who stand in the way of the Long Future, they will be shot on sight. So give me a kiss, and then I can go."

Absinthe stands, opens his poncho and envelops Turtledove. Her umbrella falls as she disappears from view, just the lower portions of her legs visible under the hem of his jacket. He holds her there, pressed against his body until she taps out.

He releases her and she steps back, wet hair strung across her face. "Helloo," she says with that angelic Turtledove smile. Then she steps forward, presses a moist kiss against his mouth and tells him. "That's you last one. You know that, don't you?"

Normally, Absinthe would have asks for one more, still. But not today. "I know."

"And you have to let me go, Absinthe."

"I know."

"Do you mean that?"

"I mean that. I understand that. And I know that in my head, my heart and my stomach."

She cups her hand on his cheek. "None of us know how to love perfectly, Absinthe. The best thing we can do is just keep trying. Just keep learning. And don't be sad."

"I will be sad."

"Then find something to occupy your mind. It won't take long before it passes. Now look at me, I'm a wee bit wet. And I really have to get going. It's corporate-busy where I am. Will you walk me the car or do you want to sit here like an overgrown mushroom?"

Posh Ones Like A Bit of Rough

Next morning, Absinthe wakes to the sound of his phone buzzing. He leans over the side of the bed and sweeps his hands around the floor until he finds it. Then he retrieves his reading glasses. He's got a sore head from the Bazooka Bar. Too many nitro-glycerine cocktails. He can't remember what happened last night, or how he got home. Nothing unusual there.

With his glasses now on, he activates his phone and finds that he has something that he has never had before. It's a video message from Turtledove. She's standing a few feet from the camera, so it's not just her face that's visible. She's dressed corporate, as ever, her beige overcoat and Louis Vuitton handbag on her arm.

She's at the airport. It seems like her flight departs imminently and she is hurried in delivering her message. "Absinthe, I didn't want your last memory of me to be bedraggled in the rain. This is how I want you to remember me." She raises her arms to flaunt her immaculate attire. "I'm going deep underground and I will probably never see you again. I'm sorry I couldn't give you what you wanted. You do deserve it. Find someone who is available. That's my advice to you. Thank you for what you have done for me. Bye-bye, Absinthe Rhinohorn. Bye-bye." She kisses her palm, and blows the kiss towards the camera. Then she steps forward and switches off the recording.

Absinthe sighs at length, mesmerized. He replays the message, staring at the little screen, taking in every little detail: what she's wearing, her jewellery, the way she moves. When it completes, he lowers the phone, and lowers his eyes. The sensation is not one of sadness, more it is a sense of a door being gently closed. He knows that he is at the back of the queue again, at the bottom of the hill. But he's not covered in mud, this time, nor is he beating himself up for being there.

He understands why is there, and he knows how to get back to where he wants to be. He sighs again, feeling the loss. He contemplates playing the message again, to distract him. But he thinks best to just let it go. "Stop chasing Turtledove," he thinks.

He sighs again, conscious of the fact that he is going to be glum for weeks. Then he notices something very strange. Something orange.

Across the room, under the chair is a pair of orange high heels. "Strange," thinks Absinthe Rhinohorn. Maybe he found them in the street last night and bought them home for a reason that only an inebriated man could understand. Then something stranger still: on the chair, there is clothing. It looks like an orange dress; some silky, shiny fabric that a barely dressed woman would wear. And what's that, on top of the dress? It looks like a frilly orange G-String.

"What the devil is going on," wonders Absinthe, most perplexed. Then he gets the odd sensation that somehow, he is not alone. It is the sense of someone's body heat radiating towards him. Cautiously, he turns and sees that there is a young woman in his bed. She's sitting upright, with her back against the wall, the bed sheet wrapped around what Absinthe can only guess is her naked body.

She says, "The posh ones like a bit of rough. But they can't handle the tumble, hey?"

"*Uh-huh?*" Absinthe is lost for words.

"Me," the woman continues, "I like the rough with the tumble. All together. I'm—"

Absinthe interrupts. "I know who you are. You are Marmalade. You looked after me in the clinic."

"That's me. How's your heart, Absinthe?"

How's his heart? It's pretty good, actually. Ever since Helmet and the new guy ventilated the Love Coin miners and blew up their computers, his pacemaker has been operating at normal speed. Sure his heart is a little heavy from all the ups and downs with Turtledove, but otherwise, it's in good shape.

"And you made me that little statue," he says, remembering the things piled on the note from the previous night.

"Did you like that?"

"I did, but I didn't know who it was."

"You do drink a lot, you know," Marmalade tells him.

"I know. I drink like a bloody fish." His eyes flicker to the bed sheets as he thinks about the long list of shortcomings that have been laid bare over the recent days. But looking at the bedsheet doesn't fix them. Only he can do that by engaging with them. "Keep trying," that's what everyone tells him. You're not well built. There will be false starts and misfires, and the occasional absolute cluster-fuck. But keep going. Start now.

Absinthe flashes one of his famous Rhinohorn smiles at Marmalade and she returns with a cheeky grin.

"I got great tits, don't I Mr Randy Horn?" she says, wiggling them provocatively under the bed sheet.

"I honestly cannot remember, Miss Marmalade," Absinthe Rhinohorn tells her. "Why don't I take another look?"

oOo